## ALSO BY WALLACE STROBY

*Cold Shot to the Heart*

*Gone 'til November*

*The Heartbreak Lounge*

*The Barbed-Wire Kiss*

# KINGS
## OF
# MIDNIGHT

# KINGS

## OF

# MIDNIGHT

*Wallace Stroby*

Minotaur Books
New York

This is a work of fiction. All of the characters, organizations, and events portrayed in this novel are either products of the author's imagination or are used fictitiously.

KINGS OF MIDNIGHT. Copyright © 2012 by Wallace Stroby. All rights reserved. Printed in the United States of America. For information, address St. Martin's Press, 175 Fifth Avenue, New York, N.Y. 10010.

www.minotaurbooks.com

Library of Congress Cataloging-in-Publication Data

Stroby, Wallace.
    Kings of midnight / Wallace Stroby.—1st ed.
      p. cm.
    ISBN 978-1-250-00037-8 (hardcover)
    ISBN 978-1-4299-5116-6 (e-book)
    1. Crime—Fiction.   2. Female offenders—Fiction.   I. Title.
PS3619.T755K56 2012
813'.6—dc23

                     2011045371

First Edition: April 2012

10  9  8  7  6  5  4  3  2  1

Some lose their life by not knowing how to save it; others, by not wanting to. . . .
The person who races through a life of vice comes to a doubly quick end.

—Baltasar Gracian,
*The Art of Worldly Wisdom*

# ONE

Crissa pulled the ski mask over her face, shifted the front-end loader into neutral, looked across the blacktop at the ATM, the redbrick bank beyond. Heat lightning pulsed on the horizon.

The loader chugged and shook around her, the vibration coming up through her boots. With a gloved hand, she cleared condensation from the windscreen. At the far edge of the parking lot, near the trees, Hollis flashed the headlights of the stolen pickup.

She worked the bucket control lever with her right hand, heard the mechanism clank and hum. The bucket rose slowly. She'd stolen the loader from a construction site a half mile away, driven it here down back roads with the headlights off. They'd chosen the bank because of its location. Woods on three sides, and a highway in front. But at 3:00 A.M., the cars were few and moving fast.

She braked, pushed the steering column lever into first gear, stepped on the throttle pedal. The loader surged forward, eager.

She tried to steer around a curb, but caught the edge, the big tires rolling over it, the cabin rising and falling.

The ATM was on a concrete island, the farthest of the three drive-through lanes. She came in at the wrong angle, had to brake, back up. The reverse sensor beeped, barely audible over the engine. As she backed and filled, she could see Hollis watching her through the windshield of the pickup, getting nervous.

She ran it in again, this time got the bucket lined up with the ATM, braked. On the screen, she could see flashing advertisements, one fading into another, the screen never dark. She raised the bucket so the bottom edge cleared the concrete island. If she misjudged, smashed the ATM rather than toppled it, she could back up, try again, but that would take more time, more exposure.

She was in range of the security cameras now, the point of no return. Her hands were clammy inside the gloves. Hollis started to ease the pickup forward, waiting for her. She let her breath out slowly, engaged the bucket safety to lock it into place, and hit the throttle.

The loader shuddered as the bucket's edge met the base of the ATM, punching into plastic and metal. The ATM groaned, tilted forward into the bucket. The screen blinked out. An alarm began to sound within the bank.

She braked, worked the bucket control. With a screech and grind, the ATM began to come away from its base. It tilted farther into the bucket, then hung there, still bound to the island with cables and framework.

Hollis was out of the pickup now, ski mask on, pry bar in hand. Crissa raised the bucket half a foot higher, sparks hissing from the shattered base. This was the risky part. If the ATM broke loose before it was fully in the bucket, it would topple back and away. It would take too much time to right it again. They would have to leave it.

She shifted into neutral, hauled on the emergency brake. Hollis had his bar wedged into the base of the ATM, working it back and forth. The machine tilted another few inches, enough for him to walk up its back face, and bear down with his weight. He jumped down then, backed away. She raised the bucket again. Resistance at first, metal screaming, and then the ATM came out of the ground all at once, trailing wires and broken masonry, crashing deep into the bucket. She heard glass pop and break.

Hollis ran back to the pickup and threw the pry bar into the bed. She backed away from the island, the beeper sounding. Bits of plastic and glass littered the blacktop. Ten feet back, she stopped, braked.

Hollis drove the pickup in front of the loader. It was a big Dodge Ram with heavy-duty suspension and an oversized bed. In this part of South Carolina, it had been easy to find. He'd stolen it from the driveway of a darkened house only an hour ago.

He got out of the pickup to direct her, waving her to adjust in one direction, then the other. When he gave her the thumbs-up and stood back, she uncurled the bucket. The ATM crashed onto its back in the truck bed, the Dodge rocking on its springs. She reversed again, watching the rearview to make sure she cleared the curb. She backed toward the trees to the spot she'd picked, where the loader couldn't be seen from the highway, then killed the engine. She pocketed the square ignition key. It was a universal fit for all John Deere loaders. This was the sixth time she had used it.

She opened the door, climbed down into the heat. Hollis had pulled the tarp down over the ATM, and was back behind the wheel of the pickup. She walked quickly to the truck, looked up into the glassy eyes of the two cameras mounted on the bank wall, then got in on the passenger side. In the distance, she could hear sirens.

They pulled away, the truck sluggish from the weight, the shocks squealing. He drove the wrong way out the entrance, bumped onto the highway.

"That one came up easier than the others," she said. She took off her mask, shoved it into a pocket of her windbreaker. Her face was damp with perspiration.

"Could have fooled me." He was watching the rearview for lights. The sirens grew louder.

"Mask," she said.

"Oh, shit."

She reached over to steady the wheel while he pulled off his mask.

"Up here," she said. "On the right." They'd rehearsed the route, but it was easy to miss the turn in the dark. He steered onto a side road that led into woods.

"You can turn on the lights now," she said. "And slow down."

He popped the headlights on, eased off the gas. His dark face glistened with sweat.

"Don't forget that mask when we're done," she said. "DNA."

"I won't." The windshield was fogging now. He leaned over the steering wheel, and wiped at the glass with a gloved hand.

"You don't need to do that," she said. She fiddled with the dashboard controls, turned on the defroster. The fan hummed, and the glass began to clear. In the harsh light of the headlamps, the trees on both sides of the road seemed to be reaching toward them.

"This thing's built for heavy loads," he said. "Handles good even with all this weight. Maybe we should keep it, use it next time."

"No way." They'd stolen a different pickup each time, abandoned it when they were done. "Last thing you want is to be driving around in a hot truck."

"We can switch out the plates."

"Forget it. Besides, there isn't going to be a next time. Not for me."

He looked at her. "What do you mean?"

"We've done this six times now, each time the same way. How long before they start staking out construction sites close to banks? Or disabling front-end loaders?"

"But we've moved around. Three different states—"

"Doesn't matter," she said. "It's only a matter of time. It was a good gig, but we played it out. Time to walk away."

"Hate to hear you say that."

They were on a hill now. The ATM slid in the bed, thumped one of the walls. He shifted into low gear. She heard the far-off rumble of thunder.

"You and Rorey want to keep working it, I'll teach you how to run a loader," she said. "It's not hard, and you've got the key. But my advice is to move on. We've all made enough from this anyway."

"Rorey," he said. "Only reason I'm working with that cracker is because of you."

She'd brought Rorey in, on the word of a contact she had in Georgia. It was Hollis's gig, but the two men he'd been using— one a laid-off heavy equipment operator—had both landed long bids on drug charges. Hollis had found the man in Georgia, who found Crissa. She'd come on board, and helped Hollis fine-tune the plan to only hit machines on Friday and Saturday nights when they were loaded for the weekend. She'd brought Rorey in as the third man, but there had been friction between the two from the start.

"Dump him," she said. "Find someone else. Rorey's an adult, he'll get over it."

"When he starts talking that good ol' boy bullshit, I like to bend that crowbar over his head. No way I'd work with him without you there."

"Then there's your answer." She looked out the window at woods passing by. The road had leveled off now, and soon she could see darkened farmhouses, fields, grain silos.

"Not too fast," she said. "You'll miss it."

She unzipped a windbreaker pocket, took out the disposable cell phone, powered it up. She dialed Rorey, and waited. When he answered, she said, "How's it look?"

"Good to go. Everything quiet. You?" If something had gone wrong on either end, their code word was "zero." It meant things had fallen apart, one way or another, to split up and keep going.

"All good," she said. "We're close."

"I'll leave the light on. See you in a few." He ended the call.

"So, what are you going to do next?" Hollis said.

"Like I said in the beginning, I was just down here to build up the nest egg. I need to head back north."

"Nice nest egg."

Each of the ATMs they'd hit had carried from $30,000 to $150,000 in tens and twenties. When Hollis had first told her about the work, she'd doubted him. The numbers sounded too high. But they'd taken $125,000 from the first machine; $80,000 from the second. At her hotel back in Columbia was a pair of suitcases containing $175,000, her split of what they'd taken so far.

"It worked out," she said. "Thanks for bringing me in."

"You made it better. Improved my game. Now I have to start from scratch."

"You'll manage."

"If I ever get up north, put something together, is there a way I can reach out to you? Someone you use up there?"

"No," she said. "Not yet. Not anymore."

She thought about Hector Suarez, dead in the trunk of his car on a Jersey City street. Cut and shot over trouble she'd brought down on him. He'd been her contact for the three years she'd lived in New York. She hadn't had another since, just a loose-knit group of people she trusted to varying degrees, none very much.

She'd settled the trouble up there, but the name she'd been using—Roberta Summersfield—had been compromised. She'd left the city with nothing but the clothes on her back and a suitcase full of cash. Since then, she'd been Linda Hendryx, the name on the forged passport and driver's license she'd kept for emergencies. The only people who knew her as Crissa Stone were back in Texas. She'd spent the first eighteen years of her life there and had fled long ago.

"Up here on the left," she said. "See the mailbox?"

"Got it."

He slowed, then turned into a gravel road that led through a tobacco field. The ATM slid in the bed again as they made the turn, bumped up the road. He switched off the headlights. At the end of the road was a big tractor barn, slivers of light leaking out from around closed doors. A flashlight blinked at them, Rorey out front, signaling the all-clear.

"Just take it easy," she said to Hollis. "We'll all be out of here in an hour. You don't ever have to see him again if you don't want to."

"With that motherfucker, it'll be too soon."

Rorey was pushing open one of the big doors. Hollis braked, waited. When the opening was wide enough, he drove through onto a concrete floor. Rorey began to push the door shut behind them.

"Pull up farther," she said. "We need room to work."

There was a single drop lamp hanging over a workbench, a pool of light on the floor beneath it. Moths fluttered around the bulb. Her rented Ford was parked on one side of the barn, out of the way, nose out. Next to it was Rorey's battered white van. Rorey had found this place, sat on it for three days to make sure it was out of use.

Hollis shut the engine off. From outside, another rumble of thunder.

"Remember what I told you," she said.

"About what?"

"Everything."

She got out. The barn smelled of oil and straw, the air heavy with humidity. Rorey came toward her. He wore a white T-shirt, his thick forearms covered with fading blue tattoos.

He played the flashlight beam into the truck bed. "How'd we do?"

"Good enough." She opened the gate, let it clank down. "Let's see what we've got."

"I heard sirens."

"Alarm went off soon as we hit the machine. But they were pretty far off. We never saw them."

Hollis got out. Rorey hopped up into the bed, pulled the tarp back to expose the smashed screen. "Let's get it out on the floor."

She climbed up beside him, went to the top of the machine, and pushed, putting her weight into it. It barely moved. Rorey jumped down, found a handhold on the bottom of the machine, and began to pull. He looked at Hollis. "You crippled?"

"Say what?"

"You heard me." Rorey let go of the machine.

"Hollis," she said. "Give me a hand up here." He looked at her, then back at Rorey. He climbed up onto the truck bed.

"Equal shares, equal work," Rorey said.

"Do not start that shit," Hollis said, not looking at him. He bent beside Crissa, and together they braced themselves against the top of the ATM.

"What shit is that?" Rorey said.

"Quit it," she said. "Let's get this thing down."

They began to push, the ATM sliding across the bed. Hollis grunted with the effort. Rorey pulled until they got the machine onto the open gate.

"Hold it there," she said. She was breathing hard. Beneath the windbreaker, her T-shirt clung in patches to her skin.

She hopped down, found a grip on the base of the machine.

"Easy now," she said to Rorey. "Let's tilt it so it lands right. Watch your feet. On my count." She looked at Hollis. "You ready?"

He nodded, bent against the machine.

"Here we go," she said. "One, two, three."

Hollis groaned, pushed, as she and Rorey pulled. The machine hung there on the gate for a moment, resisting, and then suddenly it was sliding toward them, tipping.

"Watch it!" Hollis said. They moved back fast, out of the way. The ATM crashed facedown onto the concrete, dust rising high around it.

"Jesus Christ," Rorey said. "What the hell's your problem?"

"I said 'watch it.'"

"Almost broke my Goddamn foot."

"Maybe you need to move quicker."

"I move quick enough. You want to find out?"

"Enough," she said. "If you two can stop measuring dicks for a little while, I'd like to get this done and get out of here. Rorey, get your torch."

He glared at Hollis for a moment, then turned away and went to the workbench. An acetylene tank was mounted on a hand-cart, hose wound around the gauges, the silver torch nozzle hanging. It was the only piece of equipment they'd taken from job to job. Everything else had been stolen as needed.

"Come on," she said to Hollis. "Take a walk with me."

He jumped down from the bed as Rorey wheeled the tanks over, a pair of heavy gloves under his arm. They met each other's eyes, but Hollis kept moving. Crissa opened the barn's side door, looked out into the night. The air was thick and still. Lightning flashed on the horizon.

Behind her, gas hissed as Rorey opened the valves. He pulled a crumpled pack of Marlboros from the pocket of his T-shirt, shook one out. Studying the ATM, he speared his lips with the cigarette, then pulled on the gloves, triggered the igniter. Flame leaped from the torch nozzle. He adjusted it to a thin dagger of blue and yellow, then pulled on a pair of safety goggles. He used the torch to light his cigarette, blew smoke out.

Hollis looked at him, shook his head, and turned away. Rorey walked around the ATM, picking his spot. Then he leaned over, and brought the torch to bear. Sparks began to arc past his shoulder.

When Hollis joined her, she shut the door behind them to keep the light in. They stood in the night air.

"That fucking guy," Hollis said.

"Half an hour and we're out of here."

Beyond the tobacco field, a hill sloped down into the unbroken darkness of woods. Far in the distance, they could see a cluster of flashing red, yellow, and blue lights surrounding the bank.

"There they are," Hollis said. "Looking for their money machine."

"They're too late," she said. "It's gone."

# TWO

When they went back in, the air was filled with the acrid smell of burning metal. Rorey was making a horizontal cut across the back of the ATM, the flame reflected in his goggles. Smoke rose around him.

She took the fire extinguisher from the workbench, brought it over. The steel plate of the ATM was molten red where the flame had stroked it.

Rorey straightened, and took the torch away, cigarette dangling from his lips. "Careful," he said.

She triggered the extinguisher and gave the ATM a burst of Halon. White foam hissed and bubbled when it met hot steel. She fired another burst, then stepped back. The red glow of the metal faded. Vapor drifted across the floor like fog.

Rorey's forehead was shiny with sweat. He circled the ATM like a pool player. Ash fluttered from his cigarette.

"How's it look?" she said.

"Getting there."

He leaned over, began to make a vertical cut with the torch. Sparks leaped up, died on the concrete floor. It was a job that needed a sure touch. Hollis had told her the first time his old crew cracked an ATM, the torch man had cut too deep, set the cash alight. They'd lost half of it before getting the fire out.

When Rorey took the flame away, she hit the back plate with another Halon blast. Hollis had come over and stood near the pickup, watching them.

Rorey waited for the metal to cool, then began to make a horizontal cut across the base. She stepped back as sparks angled toward her. When the cut was finished, he straightened, said, "There you go," and shut off the torch.

Two more bursts from the extinguisher, the foam sizzling. She squeezed the trigger again, swept the spray along the back of the ATM until it was covered in white. "That should do it." She set the extinguisher down.

"Give it a couple minutes," Rorey said. He pulled the gloves and goggles off, swept a wrist across his eyes.

Hollis got two pry bars from the truck bed, handed her one. He pulled the tarp down, spread it out a few feet from the ATM.

Rorey shut off the valves, wound the hose and torch around the tank. He hung the goggles on the valve wheel, the gloves atop it, flipped his cigarette away, then stood with his hands on his hips. All three of them looking down at the cooling machine.

"Good enough," she said. She wanted to be out of there.

She drove the wedge end of the pry bar into the vertical cut, pushed down, leaning into it. The steel plate began to buckle. Hollis drove his bar in beside hers. They pulled in different directions, peeling back the two halves of the plate, the metal squealing. She could see the innards of the machine now: circuit boards, wires, and long silver racks full of cash.

"That's the shit," Hollis said.

She gave a final pull on the bar, widening the hole. Faint smoke drifted out. Hollis stepped back.

"There it is, boy," Rorey said. "Go get it."

Hollis looked at him. He was still holding the pry bar. Rorey met his eyes.

"Knock it off, both of you," she said. "Hollis, pull that tarp closer."

He set the bar down, tugged the tarp toward her. Kneeling, she wedged her bar into the aluminum cash rack, snapped it with one hard jerk. Cash slid out of the rack and down into the machine. A good haul, she thought. Maybe the best yet.

She put the bar down and began to pull stacks of bills from the machine, lining them up on the tarp.

"Get your bags," she said. "Let's do this, and get out of here."

Rorey went to his van. To Hollis, she said, "Yours is in the trunk. Car's unlocked. Get mine, too." She'd driven him to get the pickup, would drop him at his motel before heading back to Columbia.

She took more money from the machine, pulled apart two twenties that had stuck together, looked at the serial numbers. Different series, different years. The bills were mostly new, all twenties and tens, none of them sequenced. They'd gotten lucky. ATMs were unpredictable. You never knew what was in them until you cracked them. And then it was too late.

She retrieved the last of the bills from inside the mechanism. None of them was singed.

"Good work," she said to Rorey. He set an olive drab duffel bag down, undid the drawstring. Hollis came over with two suitcases, one of them hers.

Sitting cross-legged on the tarp, she began to count the money, setting the stacks aside as she was done with them. Hollis picked up the piles she'd counted, counted them again. It was their system.

When she was done, the money was spread in a fan around her, each stack about three inches high.

"One hundred and forty thousand," she said. "Four hundred and eighty."

"*Got*damn," Rorey said.

"Hollis, you get the same?"

"Oh, yeah." He was smiling. At almost forty-seven grand a share, it was their second biggest take.

She began to divide the money into three piles. Hollis was right. It was a good gig. Easy work, minimal risk, with substantial reward. No weapons, no witnesses, no one getting hurt. But it was time to move on.

Rorey began to load his money into the duffel.

"I already told Hollis," she said. "This is it for me."

Rorey looked at her as he packed the last of his money in the bag. "What do you mean?"

"I'm done with this. You should be, too. We've been to the well too many times."

"What are you talking about?" he said. "This is sweet."

"Maybe. But I'm gone anyway." She opened her suitcase, stacked cash inside. She would band the bills later, at the hotel.

Hollis had his money loaded, was latching the case.

"Maybe I'm *not* done," Rorey said. "Why do you get to decide?"

"Because I do," she said. She closed and locked her suitcase, and stood. "You get to decide, too. Like I told Hollis, you two can keep working this if you like. But I don't think it's worth it."

He looked at Hollis. "Well, isn't that just fine? You take off and leave me to work with a nigger?"

Hollis straightened and turned to face Rorey, the suitcase forgotten. "You mother*fucker*."

"Back off," she said. "Both of you."

"What'd you call me?" Rorey said.

"You heard me, bitch."

She tried to get between them, and then Rorey's hand was coming out of the duffel and there was a gun in it, a blued .45 automatic. She stepped back instinctively. He pointed it at Hollis's chest.

"Come on, nigger. You're so tough? I'm right here."

"Put that away," she said, but Rorey was ignoring her, staring at Hollis, the gun steady.

Hollis smiled, took a step back, hands on his hips. They looked at each other. There was a low echo of thunder outside.

"Don't be stupid," she said to Rorey. "Let's take our money and get away from here."

"I want to hear what else this nigger has to say first."

"Leave it. Let's go."

"Okay," Hollis said. "If that's the way it is."

She never saw him pull the gun. One second his hand was empty, the next it wasn't. It was a snub-nosed .38. He pointed it at Rorey. "There you go, cracker. That's what I've got to say."

She took another step back. The two were facing each other, less than six feet between them.

"Take a breath," she said. "We've got almost fifty grand each in front of us. All we have to do is walk out of here. Don't fuck things up. Put those guns down."

"Him first," Hollis said. He wasn't smiling anymore.

She looked from one to the other. If she could defuse the moment, it would pass.

"What are you, a couple of punk kids?" she said. " 'Him first'?

You're supposed to be pros. Knock this shit off. We're losing time."

Rorey nodded, but his gun didn't waver. Hollis raised the snubnose so it was pointed at Rorey's face.

"Okay," she said. "Now let's—"

She couldn't tell who fired first. The big .45 kicked up, Rorey already spinning away. Hollis kept firing, falling back himself. He landed hard on his side on the concrete. Rorey fell across the duffel. The echo of the shots chased itself around the barn.

"Son of a *bitch*," Hollis said.

She went to Rorey first, kicked the .45 away. He lay on his stomach, not moving. She turned him over and saw the black hole beneath his right cheekbone, just starting to ooze blood. His eyes were half open. He was gone.

Hollis coughed wetly. She crossed over to him. He was on his back now, looking up at the ceiling with wet eyes.

"Did I get him?" He coughed again.

Gently, she took the .38 from his hand. "Yeah. You got him."

"Good."

She felt the anger rising in her. "We were almost out of here."

"How bad is it?"

She pulled away the edges of his Windbreaker. The bullet had gone in the left side of his chest, the shirt there already sodden with blood. The shredded material around the hole fluttered with every breath. Sucking chest wound, she thought, a lung hit for sure.

"It's bad," she said. She put the .38 aside. He was breathing in short ragged gasps now. His chest cavity would be filling with blood.

He looked up at her. "I'm sorry," he said, and then didn't say anything more.

She stood, looked down at the two men, both still and silent now. Nothing she could do for either of them, and no telling how far the sound of the shots had traveled. It was time to go.

She pulled Rorey's duffel out from under him. There was a single spot of blood on the canvas. She dragged the bag to her rental, put it in the trunk, then went back for the suitcases. She put them in side by side, shut the lid.

She looked around the barn a final time for anything that could link her to what had happened here. There was nothing. The police would find the bodies, the guns, the gutted ATM, put two and two together. The only thing missing would be the money.

She switched off the droplight, went to the big door, and put her shoulder to it, pushed it open. On the horizon, a cloud glowed for an instant, lit from within, then went dark again.

She got behind the wheel of the Ford, started the engine, realizing only then her hands were shaking. She gripped the wheel tighter, and drove out into the darkness.

# THREE

Benny was washing pots, using a scrub brush on the last hard-ened bits of spaghetti sauce, when the two men from New York walked into the restaurant.

The kitchen door was ajar, so he had a clear view into the din-ing area. Ten tables with checkered tablecloths, the front windows fogged, the neon CAFE MILAN sign dark now. Rick, the manager, was at a table, sorting register receipts. The other tables were empty. The night had been slow, and Rick had let Pablo, the bus-boy, and Lila, the waitress, go home early.

Rick looked up from the receipts. "Sorry, fellas. We're closed. I was just about to lock the door."

The men looked around, didn't speak.

Benny was forearm-deep in hot soapy water. He dried his hands on a dish towel, got his glasses from the counter. The lenses were steamed. He wiped them clear with an edge of apron, worked the wire frames over his ears.

One of the men was in his sixties, wearing an expensive overcoat, his thick silver hair swept up and back. It took Benny a moment to realize he was looking at Danny Taliferro, older now, thinner. Under the coat, he wore a roll-top sweater that covered his throat. Still vain about that scar after all these years, Benny thought.

The other man was younger, late twenties, thigh-length leather jacket, close-cut dark hair. Benny didn't know him, just the type.

Rick stood, the kid trying to be polite. "Sorry, but the kitchen's shut down, and the grill's cold. Couldn't make you anything if we wanted to."

Taliferro looked past him. Benny backed away, kept an angle on the door.

"There's a twenty-four-hour Denny's out by the highway," Rick said. "Just a couple miles away. I can tell you how to get there. Probably the only place open this time of night."

Taliferro turned to the other man. "What did I tell you? Bumfuck, USA." Then to Rick, "We're not here to eat." An edge of hoarseness in the voice, unmistakable. Danny Taliferro for sure.

So this was it, after all this time. Benny looked around. There was a cleaver hanging above the cutting board. He set it on the counter, covered it with the dish towel. Almost immediately, he felt foolish. What was he going to do, go out there swinging?

"We're looking for Benny Roth," Taliferro said. "He works here, right?"

"Who?" Confusion in Rick's voice. Benny stayed where he was, listening.

"Benny Roth," Taliferro said. "But maybe he calls himself something else now, right? I guess he would."

The kid squared his shoulders. "I don't know what you two

fellas want. But there's no Benny here. And I'd appreciate it if you all would leave now. We're closed for the night."

Benny suddenly felt guilty. The kid was going to get himself hurt over something he didn't understand.

Benny took a last glance at the dish towel, then pushed open the kitchen door. The three turned to look at him. Taliferro smiled.

"Benny," he said. "Long time."

Rick looked from Benny back to the men. "Leonard, you know these guys?"

Taliferro laughed. "Leonard?"

"It's okay," Benny said. "Yeah, I know them." He took off his apron, bundled it. "We're good in there. I did the last of the pots, loaded the washer. It just needs to be turned on."

"What's all this 'Benny' stuff?" Rick said.

"What?" Taliferro said. "You didn't know you had a celebrity working for you?"

Benny set the apron on a table. "How you doing, Danny?"

Taliferro nodded, looked him over. "Day at a time, like everybody. What's it been? Twenty-five years?"

"Longer," Benny said.

"You got old."

"We all did."

"What's all this about?" Rick said.

Benny touched his arm. "It's all right." Then to Taliferro, "How about we talk outside? Let this man finish closing his restaurant."

Taliferro swept an arm toward the door. "After you."

"Leonard . . ." Rick said.

"It's okay," Benny said. "I'll see you in the morning." To Taliferro, he said, "I just need to get my coat."

"I'll go with you," the younger one said.

"No need for that," Taliferro said. "I don't think we're gonna have any issues here."

Benny went back into the kitchen, got his red hunter's jacket from the peg, looked at the dish towel, then the back door. He could make a run for it, but wouldn't get far with his bum knee. And there might be more of them outside, waiting. It would only piss them off if he tried to get away.

When he came back out, the younger one was holding the door open.

"Maybe I should call the sheriff's office," Rick said.

"No," Benny said, pulling on his coat. "These are friends from back home. I haven't seen them in a long time."

"Back home?" Rick said. "St. Louis?"

"Somewhere like that," Taliferro said. "Come on, let's go have a drink."

Benny zipped his coat, and they went out into the cold. There was a shiny Lincoln Town Car with New York plates parked at the curb, just behind his own Hyundai. Except for the Sunoco station two blocks away, all the storefronts on Main Avenue were dark.

"You two drive all the way out here?" Benny said.

"Seemed easiest," Taliferro said. He took a hard pack of Marlboros from his overcoat pocket, offered them. Benny said, "No, thanks."

Taliferro lit one with a silver Zippo, turned his head and blew out smoke. Benny looked at the younger man. "Who's this?"

"My nephew," Taliferro said. "Frank Longo. My sister's boy. You knew his father, Petey."

"Right," Benny said, lying. The name meant nothing to him. "How you doing, kid? How's the old man?"

"Dead," Longo said. "Last year. Cancer."

"Sorry to hear that."

Taliferro said, "Sal Bruno says hello."

"That psycho?" Benny said. "He still alive?"

"Better not let him hear you say that."

Rick was at the window. Benny waved to reassure him.

"I should have figured you'd be working in a restaurant," Taliferro said. "You always were a good cook."

"It's something I enjoy." Benny looked past him, toward the gas station, knew he'd never make it. "How'd you find me?"

"It was easy," Taliferro said. "Everybody knows you've been out here, since you left the program. Isn't hard to track a person down these days, Internet and all. You are out of it, right? Or was that just a rumor?"

Benny shrugged, put his hands in his pockets. "I told them to go fuck themselves."

"That's what I heard. But you lived off that federal tit a good long time, didn't you?"

"They screwed me over, made promises they didn't keep."

"What did you expect from the G, huh?" He blew out smoke. "But hey, come on, it's cold out here. Let's take a ride."

Benny looked at the Town Car. "No way. You want to go somewhere, I'll take my car, follow you."

"Jesus Christ," Taliferro said. "You've got nothing to worry about. Ride with us. We'll talk in the car, it'll save time. We'll drive you back here when we're done."

"I don't think so."

"You're gonna wanna hear what I have to say, I guarantee you."

"Come on," Longo said. "Get in the car." Benny looked at him, didn't move.

"Benny, let me explain something to you," Taliferro said. "Anyone had a beef against you is long gone. Why do you think nobody's bothered you all this time? And you stood up to the feds, told them to go pound sand. You got some respect back for that."

"I never testified against you or your people," Benny said. "I did what I had to do, nothing more."

"I know that. Got their money's worth out of you though, didn't they? Put you on the circuit."

"They didn't give me a choice. You think I wanted that?"

"I don't know what you wanted. Couldn't any of us figure out what was in your head, everything we'd done for you."

"Done for me? You mean done *to* me?" Benny said. "With that crazy Jimmy Burke going around whacking everybody? I was next on his list. The feds played me the tapes to prove it."

"Freezing my nuts off out here," Longo said. "Can't we do this in the car?"

"The feds, they like to fuck with you," Taliferro said. "That's how they get into your head, make you do things you know are wrong."

"Maybe," Benny said.

"Anyway, they're all gone now, that crew. Jimmy, Paulie, Tommy. All dead. Couple others went into the program. For all I know, they're dead, too. If anybody wanted you, Benny, they'd have found you. The world's not that big."

"What about Joey Dio? He's still around."

"Not anymore," Taliferro said. "That's what I want to talk to you about. Come on, the kid's right. It's freezing out here. Get in."

"Do I have a choice?"

"Of course," Taliferro said. "You always got a choice."

Longo drove, Taliferro riding shotgun. Benny sat behind, left arm across the seat back, trying to act casual. He'd refused to get in front.

"So," Taliferro said. "Leonard?"

"It fits. I'm half Jewish, remember? Not that they can tell a Jew from an Italian out here anyway."

They were on a long straight road, dark fields on both sides. Benny caught a glimpse of the moon through the clouds.

"All this open space makes me nervous," Taliferro said. "How'd you end up out here anyway?"

"They had me in a bunch of different places. When I signed out of the program, I decided to stay in Indiana. I like it here."

"That's hard to believe." Taliferro turned toward him. "Things didn't work out with the wife, eh?"

"You heard that, too?"

"Some of it."

"She's gone now."

"I know. I was sorry to hear about that. You ever see your kids?"

"Why do you ask?"

"Just curious."

"Not for a long time. They're grown now. In college, I think. Hope."

A deer came out of the woods ahead of them, eyes flashing in the headlights. Longo hit the brakes hard, and they were all thrown forward for an instant, then back. The deer bounded across the road, disappeared into the trees on the other side.

"Son of a bitch," Longo said. "Sorry about that, skip. I didn't see it."

"We're fine. Just take it easy."

They drove on.

"Where are we going?" Benny said.

Taliferro looked back at him. "Your place."

Benny stiffened. "What do you mean?"

"I told you it wasn't hard to track you down, find where you live. You got a nice thing going there, huh? How old's that girl? Twenty-five? Good for you."

Benny sat forward. "Wait a minute . . ."

"Relax," Taliferro said. "So I know a little bit about you. No big deal. You think I was going to drive all the way out here, not know what I was getting into?"

"She's got nothing to do with what happened before."

"Did I say she did? But you're like, what, sixty, sixty-one?"

"Sixty-two."

"And she's twenty-five? When I heard that, I said 'God bless America.'"

"And pass the Viagra," Longo said.

"Be nice," Taliferro said. Then, over the seat to Benny, "This is the turn up here, right?"

"You been here before?"

Taliferro didn't answer. They made a left into the driveway, gravel crunching under the tires.

All the lights in the house were on. That was wrong. Marta would have turned them off. They barely made their rent each month, and every dollar counted.

"I thought we were going to talk in the car," Benny said. "Then you were gonna drive me back."

"We're here now," Taliferro said. "Might as well be comfortable."

They pulled up outside the porch. Only ten o'clock, but the houses on both sides were dark. The only sound was wind in the trees.

"You own this place?" Taliferro said, but Benny was already out of the car. The front door was unlocked, the living room empty.

He went into the kitchen, and Marta was sitting there at the table, arms crossed. Relief flooded through him, and then he saw the other man there, leaning against the kitchen counter. He was Longo's age, but thicker, a weight lifter's body, spiky moussed hair. He wore a leather coat over an open shirt, a gold cross gleaming in his chest hair.

"What the fuck?" Benny said.

"Ease up," Taliferro said from behind him. "Everything's okay. We're just here to talk."

"Benny, what is this?" she said. She was scared, but the anger was coming through. She wore a green flannel shirt, white T-shirt beneath. Her straw-colored hair was tied back.

"Baby, are you all right?" he said.

She pushed back her chair, started to stand, and the third man put a hand on her shoulder. She pulled away from him. "Benny, who are these people?"

"Everybody relax," Taliferro said. To the third man, Taliferro said, "She's okay, Dominic, right? Nothing happened?"

"It's all good," he said. "But she don't like me much."

Benny turned to Taliferro. "This is out of line."

"I had a look around," Dominic said. He took Benny's stubby Colt .380 from a coat pocket. "Found this in the nightstand."

"Huh," Taliferro said. "Can't blame him." He squeezed Benny's shoulder. "It's okay. Trust me." Then to Dominic, "Why don't you take the young lady out into the living room, so Benny and I can talk?"

"This isn't right," Benny said.

"Easier this way," Taliferro said. "You got some coffee or something you can fix? Maybe a drink, warm us up?"

Dominic put the Colt back in his pocket, said, "Come on, honey."

She looked at Benny.

"The sooner we talk," Taliferro said, "the sooner we're on our way."

Benny nodded at her. When Dominic tried to take her elbow, she pulled away. He backed off, raised his hands in mock surrender. She went past them, down the hall and into the living room. Dominic followed.

"She'll be all right," Taliferro said.

Benny felt Longo come up behind him. He patted the sides of his coat, reached around, felt his waist.

"This is bullshit, Danny," Benny said, feeling the first stirrings of panic.

"Sorry, but we didn't want you going rabbit on us when we showed up. How much does she know?"

"About what?"

"About you."

"Does it matter?"

"She knows your real name at least. None of that 'Leonard' bullshit."

"I met her out here. She's got nothing to do with back home."

"Of course not. Now let's all sit down, have a drink."

Longo pulled out a chair for Benny. Taliferro took the one across the table. He sat back, and the collar of his sweater slid down an inch. Benny could see the thin, welted scar just above the Adam's apple, where the piano wire had cut through flesh.

"I've got tea, coffee," Benny said. "No alcohol."

"Why not?"

"I haven't had a drink in six years."

"No booze, no cigarettes. Congratulations. Living clean."

"Trying to."

"I admire that. Wish I could."

He got the Marlboros out again, lit one with the Zippo. Longo leaned back against the counter, where Dominic had been. The right side of his jacket hung heavy.

Taliferro blew out smoke, nodded at the hallway. "Sorry about all this. Can't blame her for being angry, I guess. Us just showing up like that, out of the blue."

"What is it you want?"

He tapped ash on the floor. "I guess you didn't hear the news?"

"If it's about Joey Dio, no. What happened?"

"He's gone. They let him out of Springfield about a month ago, sent him home. Brain tumor. Nothing they could do about it. Miracle he lived as long as he did."

"I should cry?"

Taliferro smiled. "Yeah, Joey could be a difficult guy. Never really gave a shit about anyone except himself. Like they used to say, he always ate alone."

Benny said nothing, waited.

"He went straight into hospice when he got out. Only lasted a couple weeks though. It was in all the papers back home. Surprised you didn't hear about it out here."

"I didn't. What's this got to do with me?" Sensing already where it was headed.

"You and Joey went way back. Everyone knew that, respected it."

"He tried to have me killed. He gave the order."

"Yeah, he could be that way. I hardly knew the man, but I still had to kick up to him. Every crew in Brooklyn and Queens did. It always burned me."

"You and everybody else," Benny said.

"You're right. But the thing with Joey, what no one could ever figure out, was that airport deal."

"The what?" Knew for certain now.

"Lufthansa. Your buddy Jimmy the Gent. You were part of that crew, right? Biggest score of all time back then. That's wise-guy mythology now. They still talk about it on the street."

"That was thirty-five years ago. And I had nothing to do with it anyway. I'm going to make coffee. You want some?"

"Sure. That sounds good."

Benny looked at Longo, who shook his head. Benny got up, went to the sink, filled the coffeemaker with water from the faucet, got it going.

"Yeah, it was a long time ago," Taliferro said. "Still, most of that money never turned up. Anyway, why am I telling you this? You know more about it than I ever will."

"If that's what you heard, don't believe it." He got mugs down from the cabinet. "Way I heard it, that money got whacked up as soon as it left the airport. All the bosses between here and Florida got a piece. You want milk, sugar?"

"What I heard, too, and where some of it went," Taliferro said. "Yeah, sugar, thanks. But word was Joey kept almost half of it for a rainy day. He was so greedy, he wouldn't let anyone near it. So he sat on it all those years."

"I wouldn't know."

The coffee began to percolate. Benny got sugar packets from a ceramic jar, tore them open and emptied two into each mug. Longo was leaning against the counter with his arms crossed, watching him.

"You hear wild figures all the time," Taliferro said. "About how much they took out of there. Six million, eight million, ten million. Figure gets higher every year. What do you think it was?"

Benny shrugged, waiting on the coffee. "Maybe less. Maybe

five in cash, some more in jewelry. Who knows? Everybody who did is dead."

"Not everybody."

"Most of them."

"You never got a cut?"

"I was with Jimmy's crew when it happened, that's all. Jimmy took his share, doled some of it out, kicked the rest up to Joey. That job made some guys rich, but mostly it made them dead. It almost got me killed, and I never saw a dime of it."

"That's hard to believe."

"Believe what you want."

Benny leaned back against the counter, wondered if Taliferro had a gun as well.

"Way I figure it," Taliferro said, "you might know where Joey hid that money. Or at least have a pretty good idea."

Benny tried to laugh. "I wish."

"Then we got a problem here."

"What's that?"

"I don't believe you."

The coffee was ready. Benny took the glass pot off the burner, poured some into the mugs.

"Joey didn't trust anyone," he said. "Not even his own people. Why would I know where he stashed his money? If he did in the first place, which I doubt."

"He wouldn't have to tell you, for you to know," Taliferro said. "You were the smartest one in that crew. You're the only one still standing, right?"

Benny weighed the coffeepot in his hand. It was still half full. He put it back on the burner, opened a drawer. The Ginsu paring knife was where it always was, beside the cutlery tray. He took a teaspoon out, stirred the coffee in the mugs, left the drawer half open. He tossed the spoon in the sink.

"Got some cookies somewhere if you want them." He put Taliferro's mug on the table. "Chips Ahoy, I think."

"Stop screwing around. Talk to me."

Benny sat back down, sipped his coffee. It singed his tongue. He rolled the mug between his hands to warm them, limber up his fingers, Taliferro watching him.

"Here's the deal," Benny said. "I don't know where that money is, or even if it exists. And if it did—a big if, by the way—I wouldn't even know where to start looking."

"It didn't go far, I'd bet. Joey never had much imagination. He knew the city, that's all."

"Then it's probably in a bank somewhere. Safe deposit box."

Taliferro shook his head. "He wouldn't leave it someplace the G might get it. No, it's stashed somewhere, probably all of it in one place. That's the way he was."

"Then you know more about it than I do," Benny said. He drank coffee.

Taliferro rocked back on his chair. "Well, then, like you said, here's the deal. I think you know more than you're telling. We can stay out here as long as we need to, and find out. Or we can take you back with us, whether you want to go or not. The girl too. Put you in the fucking trunk if we have to."

"Nice. That's the way you ask for my help?"

"I'm through asking. Way I look at it, you've got two ways to go. Come with us, help us look, maybe get a taste of that money. Or keep shining me along, and we'll find out what you know anyway, leave you in a cornfield somewhere. And you won't be alone."

"Not much of a choice."

"Maybe not. But there it is."

Benny got up, took his mug to the counter. "If I go back with you, what do I have to do?"

"Ask around. Talk to some of those old-timers you know. Take us around some places."

"Maybe somebody's already found it."

"No, I would've heard. Besides, no one had the balls to look for that money when Joey was still alive. Everybody was too scared of him. But now he's gone, people are gonna *start* looking. We get there first, you get a nice piece of it."

"That might work out," Benny said. "If I get some assurances."

"Assurances? Don't overestimate your position here."

Benny smiled, filled his mug again. Steam rose from the cup.

"Don't worry about that," he said. "After all these years, one thing I've learned is to see things as they are."

"There you go," Taliferro said. "Like I said, smart."

Taliferro picked up his mug with his right hand, and Benny knew this was his best chance. He turned fast, still holding the coffeepot, swung it wide and into Longo's forehead.

The pot exploded, and glass and coffee flying. Longo cried out, fell back against the counter, hands at his face. As he went down, Benny took the paring knife from the drawer, turned just as Taliferro began to stand, with his right hand going into his overcoat pocket.

He shoved the knife into Taliferro's right shoulder, just above the armpit. The point went in two inches, hit something hard. Taliferro grunted, pulled at the hilt with his left hand, tangled in his chair and went over backward.

Benny knelt beside Longo, heard Dominic coming down the hall. He flung a wild elbow back, caught Longo in the face, then pushed a hand into his jacket pocket, felt the pistol he'd hoped was there. His hand closed around it, finger on the trigger.

Dominic stood in the kitchen doorway, gun in hand. Benny tilted Longo's gun up inside the pocket, hoped it didn't have to be cocked first.

Dominic looked around the room, confused, then at Benny, just as he squeezed the trigger.

The shot was loud. Material blew out of the jacket, and Dominic's left leg went out from under him. He hit the floor hard.

Longo's arm locked around Benny's throat, pulled him back. Benny tugged at the gun. It snagged inside the pocket for a moment, then came free, a chromed automatic.

Longo clawed at Benny's eyes, sent his glasses flying. Benny twisted away, hit him twice across the bridge of the nose with the butt of the gun, then again in the right temple. Longo's eyes lost focus. He fell onto his side.

Benny scrambled away, stood, breathing heavy. Dominic had dropped his gun, was holding his left leg with both hands. Benny swept the gun away with his foot, sent it skittering into a corner. He leaned over, reached into Dominic's coat pocket, took out his own Colt, stood back, a gun in each hand.

Taliferro had the knife out, his hands slick with blood. He was on his knees, but moving slow, his face white. Lucky shot, Benny thought. Through the overcoat and all, he'd hit something important.

He stuck Longo's gun in his coat pocket. Marta was in the doorway, watching him.

"What happened?" she said. "Are you all right?"

Taliferro stayed on his knees, left hand holding his right shoulder. Longo was still motionless, slumped against the counter. Benny looked around, found his glasses, put them back on. The frames were bent, but the lenses intact.

"You motherfucker," Dominic said. "You son of a bitch." He

was holding his leg just above the knee, blood coming through his fingers.

Marta went past him, got his gun from the corner. She pointed it at him, her finger tight on the trigger.

"No," Benny said. "Don't." He was breathing hard, had trouble getting the words out. He put a hand over the gun she held, guided it down and away, Dominic watching them. She let Benny take it.

"Get the suitcases," he said. "Start putting some clothes together. For both of us. Quick as you can."

"Are you okay, baby?"

"I'm good. Go on." He stuck Dominic's gun in his belt.

When she was gone, Benny looked at Taliferro and said, "I should kill all three of you."

"You have not got the balls."

Benny's glasses began to slide. He pushed them back up his nose. They were still crooked.

Longo groaned. Benny looked at him, then back at Taliferro. "You got a gun in that pocket?"

Taliferro spit on the floor. "Come over here and find out."

The Colt started to tremble. Benny steadied it with his other hand.

"If you're going to shoot," Taliferro said, "then shoot."

After a moment, Benny lowered the gun. He righted a chair, sat down, tried to catch his breath.

Everything was fucked. It was trouble to leave these three alive. They wouldn't give up now, wouldn't leave him alone. But he couldn't kill them, not like this.

Marta came into the kitchen. "There aren't enough suitcases. We've only got the two."

"Pack what we can carry," he said. "Forget about the rest."

When she turned, he said, "Wait a minute. Find some rope. Clothesline, anything. Check the hall closet."

When she went out, Taliferro said, "Where do you think you're going to run to? You and that little whore?"

"Shut up." Benny stood. His right elbow ached where he'd hit Longo. He could hear Marta out there rooting in the closet.

Taliferro and Dominic were watching him. Longo began to stir. Benny knew he was running out of time.

"You ever fire that thing before?" Taliferro said. "Doesn't look like it, the way you're holding it."

"Shut up," Benny said again, feeling foolish now. Marta came back in with a ball of recycling twine, handed it to him. It would have to do.

Benny went around the table, kicked the bloody paring knife aside. He gestured at Taliferro with the Colt. "On your stomach."

"Screw you."

Benny raised the gun, fired into the wall over Taliferro's head. The gun kicked up like a live thing in his hand, the bullet slapping a hole through the sheetrock. Taliferro flinched, leaned away. Dust drifted down on him.

Benny lowered the muzzle, pointed it at Taliferro's face. His arm was still tingling from the recoil. "Don't make me do it, Danny."

Taliferro blinked. "You just made the biggest mistake of your life, you know that?"

"On your stomach, Danny. Don't make me shoot."

Taliferro looked at Benny, then at Marta standing behind him.

Slowly, he turned over, lay facedown. "We'll find you. You think we won't?"

Benny put the Colt on the table where he could reach it, got the twine. He knelt on Taliferro's legs, pulled his hands behind his back, wound the twine six times around his wrists. He got the paring knife, cut the loose line, tied it tight. Taliferro winced.

"You're making this worse for both of you," he said. "If you're smart, you'll just walk away now."

Benny patted his overcoat pockets. No gun.

"Shut up," he said. "Don't make me change my mind."

Benny did his ankles next, then cut a length of twine, moved to Longo. Dominic was watching him, but his eyes were heavy. The pool of blood under his leg was spreading.

Longo groaned again when Benny rolled him onto his stomach, tied his wrists. Concussion, Benny thought, or worse. Longo kicked out weakly, and Benny pinned his legs, tied his ankles. He went through his pockets, found the Lincoln keys.

"Finish packing, get the bags," he said to Marta. "We need to go. Now." She went out.

Dominic's eyes were half-closed now. Passing out from blood loss, Benny thought.

Benny felt light-headed, had to sit down again, catch his breath. The room seemed to swim around him.

Taliferro had twisted to face him. Benny tried to steady his breathing, waited until the room slowed. He took off his glasses, straightened the frames as much as he could, put them back on. He looked around the room, and it all settled in on him now, what he had just done. He used a sleeve to wipe sweat from his brow.

Marta came back with two suitcases, an overnight bag.

"Got everything you need?" he said.

"Are we really going?"

"We have to." He tossed the keys. She caught them in midair. "Put our stuff in their car. We'll drive it downtown, get mine. We're not coming back."

When she went out, he stood again, steadier now, breathed deep.

"Sooner or later, you'll work your way free," he said to Taliferro. "First thing you should do is call nine-one-one. Your friend Dominic's not in such good shape."

"Don't you worry about him."

"I'm not. I just don't want a dead man on my tab, if I can avoid it."

"You'll get yours, too, you Jew bastard. Bet on it."

"I know I will," Benny said. "Everybody does."


They left town on Route 70, heading east. Outside Cloverdale, Benny pulled over, tossed the two guns and the Lincoln keys over a fence and into a retention pond. The Colt was in his suitcase.

He kept an eye on the rearview as he drove. For what, he wasn't sure. It wouldn't be the Town Car. Even if they had an extra set of keys, he'd flattened all four tires.

They drove in silence. After an hour, they began to see signs for Ohio. The Hyundai still had a half tank of gas.

"Where are we going?" Marta said.

"New York. Brooklyn, maybe. I'm not sure yet."

"New York? Isn't that where those men are from?"

"Yeah."

"Then why are we going there?"

"There are people I know there. Down in Jersey, too. They might be able to help us."

"When are we coming back?"

He squeezed her thigh. "We're not, baby. I'm sorry."

"My parents."

"When we get settled, you can call them. But not until then. Better they don't know anything, in case someone comes around to talk to them."

"Who?"

"I don't know. Police, probably. Maybe someone else."

"Are they in danger?"

"No," he said. "Of course not. Why would they be?" Wishing it were true.

He was feeling light-headed again, weightless. "Did you bring my Monopril?"

"It's in your bag, I'll get it. Are you okay? Feeling dizzy?"

"I'm fine. I just forgot to take it today." Lying again.

She leaned over the seat, fumbled with the overnight bag. She came back with the pill bottle, opened it, shook a tablet into her palm.

"Thanks." He took it from her and dry-swallowed it, winced at the bitter taste.

Ahead of them, clouds were thinning, stars showing through.

It's all come down to this again, he thought. On the road. On the run. Maybe the way it'll always be. For the rest of his life, running.

"My parents warned me," she said.

"About what?"

"You. That you would get in trouble again. That someday you'd go back where you came from, leave me behind."

"Did you believe them?"

"No."

"Good. Because wherever I'm going, baby, you're coming with me. I promise you."

She took his hand in both of hers, leaned into his shoulder.

"Go ahead and sleep," he said. "We've got at least an hour before we have to stop for gas. Are you hungry?"

"Not yet."

"Let me know when you are. I'll stop."

She closed her eyes. Then, barely above a whisper, she said, "I'm scared."

"I am, too. But everything's going to be all right."

She squeezed his hand tighter. "I love you."

"I love you, too, angel," he said. "And don't worry. I'm never gonna let you go."

She nestled into him, warm against his shoulder. In minutes, she was asleep.

He drove on into the night.

# FOUR

Crissa took an Amtrak train as far as Baltimore, got a cab to a hotel near the Inner Harbor. The bellboy loaded her two suitcases and overnight bag on a luggage cart. She followed him into the elevator, rode up to the fifth floor. The overnight held clothes, a laptop she'd bought in Atlanta, and a .32 Beretta Tomcat. The suitcases were full of money.

When he was gone, she opened the suitcases on the bed, spent the next half hour counting and banding bills. She was exhausted, kept losing her place and having to start over again.

When she was done, the stacks of cash were laid out neatly on the bed. The total came to $340,560. Some of it was left over from the stake she'd had back in December, but most of it came from the six ATMs. Even though the bills weren't sequenced, she'd have to find a way to launder them, to be safe. Hollis had a man in Savannah ready to handle it for them, but she'd had no contact with him. Only Hollis knew who he was. Now, with Hollis gone, the problem was her own.

She put the money back in the suitcases. She knew little about Rorey or Hollis, whether they had family, children. They'd only come together to do the work. Even if she were able to find their people, hand over their shares, it would be too much risk. The money was hers now.

There was an arena across the street, the neon glow from its facade lighting the room. She closed the heavy curtains to shut it out, then pulled off her boots, lay on the bed.

She'd make some phone calls from here. Then head north, try to reconnect with Rathka, the lawyer in New York. She thought of Wayne in prison in Texas, his parole hearing coming up in just a few weeks. With Rathka's help, she'd already funneled more than a quarter million in cash to a lawyer in Austin, who had an inside man at the statehouse with influence on the parole board. But it wasn't a sure thing. Nothing was.

The identity she'd left behind in New York was the one she'd used to get on the approved visitors roll at the prison in Kenedy. The name was on file there, along with her photo. She couldn't go back. Wayne was pushing fifty-one, with seven years left on an armed-robbery bid. Being inside was killing him. If he didn't get out soon, she knew, she might never see him again.

She closed her eyes, the fatigue on her. She felt suddenly alone, adrift. Less than twenty-four hours since she'd left Rorey and Hollis, dead on a cold concrete floor. A stupid waste of life. There'd been too much blood lately, too many bodies.

She'd killed a man in December, a man who'd taken out two of her partners, nearly crippled a third. That one man had undone everything she'd built. She'd shot him to death outside a burning house in Connecticut, left him there in the snow. It was the first life she'd ever taken. The killing had drawn police from two states, and brought an end to the life she knew.

Now it was time to build again. Everything she owned in the world was in that hotel room. There was nothing else. She would use the money to carve out another life, find a place to call home. A new start with Wayne, far away from steel doors and razor wire. A beginning.

She was too tired to shower or undress. That could wait. For now, everything could wait. She closed her eyes, and let sleep drag her down.

The next morning was gray, cold March rain slanting down from a leaden sky. She bought a prepaid cell phone at a corner market, took it back to the room. Standing at the window, curtains open, she called Rathka's number. Cars splashed by in the street below, people hurrying along the sidewalk.

She waited while Monique, his secretary, put her through.

"Ms. Hendryx, good to hear from you," Rathka said. "I was hoping you'd call."

"First chance I've gotten. Work's been busy."

"It's been a long time. I was worried."

The Roberta Summersfield name had led police to Rathka's office. He'd been questioned, but it had gone no further. Still, she knew he'd be reluctant to meet again, pick up where they'd left off.

"Things are fine," she said. "I was down south for a while, but the weather turned suddenly. Thought it was a good idea to leave."

"I'm sorry to hear that. I hope there were no lingering effects."

"None I'm aware of yet."

"That's good. However, I'm not sure this is the best time for further investments, the way the market is and all. Still a certain amount of turbulence."

"I understand. I wouldn't put you in that position. But I wanted an update on that other matter."

"Of course. I've been staying on top of that, even in your absence."

"And?"

"Nothing very new. Board meets on the twenty-eighth."

"Everything in place down there?"

"I wouldn't say 'in place,' but we certainly came through on our share of the deal."

"Are they asking for more?" she said.

"Not yet. I don't expect them to, either. But there's always a certain amount of risk involved, as you know. We won't know anything for sure until that day."

"I haven't been able to get down there."

"For obvious reasons."

"I can't contact him at all, not the way I used to. I don't think it's safe."

"It's not," he said. "I'd recommend you continue to act under that assumption."

"But I need to get a message to him. To let him know I'm okay. That we're working on it."

"I understand." She could hear him tap a pencil on his desktop. She was used to the pauses, the tapping. It meant he was thinking.

"Here's an idea," he said after a moment. "As one of his attorneys of record, I could arrange a phone call. It would have to be done from here, of course."

"Is that safe?"

"Safe enough, I'd think. After their initial visit here, our friends seem to have lost interest. I've had no contact with them since. So, if you're asking about the integrity of the line, I think we're fine on that."

"Good."

"I have someone come in and sweep once a month, too, as you know. And as far as the phone call, even if there was an issue, it wouldn't do them any good. Attorney-client privilege."

"Then let's do it."

"Can you get up here? How far away are you?"

"About four hours," she said. "I can rent a car, be there tomorrow. I have something for you as well. For investment purposes."

"That might be an issue right now. But we'll talk about it when I see you, examine our options. This number good for a while?"

"Yes. It's new."

"The call may take a couple days to set up. They don't move very fast down there. Let me work on it, and I'll get back to you as soon as I can."

"I'll wait to hear from you." She ended the call.

She'd planned to stay in Baltimore a few days, try to decompress from the last week. She knew no one in the city, had anonymity here. But now she was restless. She considered driving up to Atlantic City, hitting the casinos, trying to launder some of the money through chips. She could play blackjack or roulette long enough to make it look good before she cashed out. But it would take a while, and she was an indifferent gambler. It held no appeal for her.

There was a local phone book in the desk drawer. She got the number of a car rental agency, made the call. It would feel better to be on the move. There were plans to be made, to try to get her life back to where it had been. It would take time. And there was never enough of that.

\* \* \*

She left Baltimore in a Ford Fusion that afternoon, headed up I-95. She stopped in Wilmington, Delaware, and used her ID to rent safe deposit boxes at two different downtown banks. She'd bought a shoulder bag, used it to carry banded cash into the banks. In each box, she left $20,000.

She did the same at three banks in Philadelphia, then crossed the bridge into Jersey, hit two banks in Camden, two more in Trenton. It was dark by the time she got on the New Jersey Turnpike, headed north, wipers on against the drizzling rain. She had $160,000 left.

It felt good to be on the road again, moving forward, seeding cash along the way. The first steps of a new life. The rest of the money she would try to launder, keep fluid. The money in the safe boxes was for emergencies.

She tuned in a classical station. "Venus" from Holst's *The Planets* came through the speakers. It was one of the first classical CDs she'd ever bought, knew almost every note of it by heart. When she'd left New York, she'd had to leave all her music behind as well, except for what was on her laptop. Once she got settled, she'd buy more. Maybe a book, too, one of those classical guides for beginners. She could recognize favorite pieces, but beyond that she was lost.

She turned up the volume. Music filled the car, calmed her.

The rain was coming down harder now, slashing through her headlight beams, the wipers clicking rhythmically. Her hips ached, another souvenir from Connecticut, when she been clipped by a car driven by the man she'd killed. But despite the weather, despite her fatigue, somehow it all felt right. The night, the road, the music. It felt like going home.

# FIVE

When they reached the corner of Fifth Avenue and Fifty-fourth Street, Crissa told the cabdriver to pull over. They were five blocks short of the address she'd given him. He steered into the loading zone in front of the building, horns sounding behind him. She looked up at Rathka's office window, twelve stories above, and wondered if anyone beside Rathka was waiting there for her.

"Miss, I can't stay here," the driver said.

She paid him, got out. Wind was whistling down Fifth, light rain in the air. The weight of the shoulder bag pulled at her. Inside was $150,000 in cash. She'd left the other $10,000 in the trunk of the Fusion, in a parking garage downtown.

Her first time back in the city in more than three months. Rathka had given her the all-clear over the phone, but there was still the chance of a setup. Enough pressure would turn him. He had a wife, children, grandchildren, a flourishing practice. Too much to lose.

Nothing for it, though. She was here now, had nowhere else to go. She had to trust him.

When the elevator doors opened on the twelfth floor, Monique was waiting for her. She escorted her through an outer office, two of the chairs there occupied. Crissa scanned faces as she went past. A heavy black woman and a hard-looking man in his fifties, with long gray hair and a tattoo on the back of his neck. Neither of them looked much like law.

Monique led her down a hallway and into a conference room with a big oak table, law books lining the walls. Watery gray light came through the window blinds. There was a multiline phone in the center of the table.

"Can I get you something while you're waiting?" Monique said. "Coffee, tea, water?"

"Some water maybe."

There was a tray with pitcher and glasses on a sideboard. Monique brought it over to the table.

"Thanks," Crissa said. She set the shoulder bag on the table, hung her leather car coat on a chair.

"He shouldn't be long," Monique said. "He's with another client, but they're finishing up."

When she left, Crissa knelt, looked up under the table for wires, microphones. Nothing. She turned the phone over, checked the screws on the bottom for fresh marks. They were clear.

At the window, she parted the blinds, looked down at the traffic. She didn't like being up this high, not having an easy escape route.

She was still at the window when Rathka came in.

"Ms. Hendryx. So good to see you again. Sorry to keep you waiting."

He was thinner than the last time she'd seen him. Late fifties but looking older. More lines around the eyes. Dark three-piece, white shirt, red club tie.

"Walt," she said.

"Come on, let's sit down." He set a yellow legal pad on the table. "Monique's making the call. She'll buzz us when they're ready."

He poured water into a glass, ice cubes clinking in the pitcher.

"You look good," he said. "I was worried."

"Sorry for that complication."

They sat across from each other. He put the glass in front of her on a paper napkin.

"Any more fallout?" she said.

He shook his head, poured for himself. "A shot in the dark, as I said over the phone. They had nothing. I answered their questions politely, and sent them packing."

"Any feds?"

"Just locals. NYPD and Connecticut staties. Felt like there was some friction between them too. The lieutenant from Connecticut seemed to be the driving force. Very focused. But I think the city boys were looking at it as a waste of their time."

"This lieutenant, you get a name?"

He nodded, took a business card from a vest pocket, handed it over. It was blue and white, with the Connecticut state police icon in the upper right-hand corner. In embossed type, it read LT. VINCENT GAITANO, MAJOR CRIMES UNIT. There was an address, phone and fax numbers, e-mail.

"I'll keep this, if it's okay," she said.

"Be my guest. I never heard from him again, so I'm not overly concerned."

He looked at the shoulder bag, raised an eyebrow. She slid it toward him.

"I'm not sure I want to look in there," he said. "What condition is it in?"

"As found."

"That's not good."

"Couldn't be helped. Someone down there was supposed to take care of it for me. He ran into trouble."

"What kind of trouble?"

"As bad as it gets."

"That makes me even more reluctant to look."

"It's clean, as far as it goes. Can't be traced."

"You hope."

"If you don't want to deal with it, I understand. But I need to turn some of it around, to live on."

"I see, but . . ."

"There's more I've put away," she said. "I can get at it if I have to. But I need this as working capital, so I want to make sure it's clean. I've got nothing up here anymore."

"I understand. But maybe this isn't the best place for starting over."

"I don't plan to stick around. But there's no one else I can trust anymore with this. Except you."

He looked at the shoulder bag.

"A year ago, you wouldn't have thought twice about taking that money," she said.

"I'm sorry. A year ago, things were different."

The phone began to buzz. A green light blinked.

"Here we go," he said.

He picked up the receiver, listened.

"That's right," he said. "For Wayne Boudreaux. This is his attorney, Walter Rathka." A pause. "Certainly. Yes, It's cleared with all of them. Check your computer. I'll wait."

He looked at her, raised his eyebrows in a gesture of exasperation.

"Yes," he said into the phone. "I'm still here. Thank you."

Another wait. Then he said, "Wayne? This is Walt Rathka in New York. Yes, we're secure here. Are things okay on your end?"

He listened, nodded, said, "Hold on," and passed the receiver to her.

She met his eyes, took the phone, raised it to her ear.

Silence at first, then, through the phone, "Hey, darlin'."

She closed her eyes. "Hey, babe."

"I've been worried about you." His voice weaker, older.

"I'm fine," she said. "There was some trouble, but it's over."

"And you're okay?"

"Yes. I've wanted to get down to see you, but I couldn't."

"I know. Rathka told me. Don't worry about it, Red. It's better this way."

"No, it's not." She looked at the tattoo on the inside of her left wrist, the Chinese character for "perseverance." Wayne had the same on his own wrist.

"Remember what I told you the last time you were here," he said. "About moving on."

"No chance of that. We're going to get you out of there. Soon. You're short for the door."

When he didn't respond, she said, "Wayne? Are you all right?"

He coughed. "I'm fine, girl. Fine as can be. For an old man."

"Don't start that again. You're not old."

"In here I am. And older every day."

"You don't sound well."

"I've been under the weather a little, but I'm good."

"I'm not convinced."

"Forget about me. You get down to see that little girl?"

"Yes."

"Everything okay there?"

"Yes," she said. "She's good."

She had an image of Maddie, her daughter, the last time she'd seen her. At a Texas playground, laughing and running, then leaping into the arms of Crissa's cousin Leah, the woman she knew as her mother. The memory hurt.

"You need to work that out," he said. "Get her back."

"I will, someday."

He began to cough again, deep and wet.

"You're sick," she said. "Have you seen a doctor there?"

"Depends how you define doctor. Ones here barely qualify."

"I'm worried about you."

"Don't be."

"When you get out, I'll have doctors ready. The best there is. A place to live, too, for both of us."

"That sounds good." His voice flat.

"Talk to me, babe. What aren't you telling me?"

"I'm glad you could call," he said. "It's good to hear your voice."

"You'll be seeing me soon."

"Maybe. But if not, I want you to know I love you. Always did. Always will."

She blinked, felt water come to her eyes. Rathka got up, stood at the window, looking out.

"Soon you can tell me that in person," she said.

"Just in case things don't work out that way, you should know there's not a minute in here I can't close my eyes, see your face."

"I'm going down there for the hearing. I want to be around when it happens."

"No need for that."

"I want to be there."

"Worry about yourself. That's what matters now."

"What do you mean?"

"I have to go," he said. It was the way he always did it. Ending things on his own time. Not letting someone else do it, take something away from him.

"I love you," she said.

"Look after yourself, Red. That's what I want."

Clicks on the line. A dial tone sounded in her ear.

She held the receiver out. Rathka took it, replaced it in the cradle.

"Something's going on down there," she said. "Something he's not telling me."

Rathka sat again, didn't meet her eyes.

"I need to know," she said.

He sat back. "All the indicators I'm getting are positive. There are already three letters of recommendation on file. Your money's being put to good use. Don't doubt that."

"It better be."

"I'm confident they'll do everything possible. But I'm afraid there are some situations where we have to accept our powerlessness after a certain point. This is one of them."

"What are you leaving out?"

"I had my colleague down there talk to one of the guards, off the record," he said. "The guard said Wayne's been having issues with another inmate. You'll remember there was a fight last year."

"Who's the inmate?"

"Does it matter? Wayne's older than most of them in there right now. Some probably see him as an easy target. And you know Wayne, he doesn't know when to back down."

"Why should he? Is this a gang thing?"

"Isn't everything in prison?"

"Whites or Mexicans?"

"White. Aryans."

"Wayne never had much use for them. How come he hasn't been moved to another unit?"

"They offered protective custody, but he refused. That guard's keeping an eye on him, though. He'll keep us informed, try to watch out for him if he gets in another jam."

"How much is that costing?"

"It came up while you were away, so I went ahead. Not much. Ten grand so far. Just enough to keep the pump primed, give us some eyes and ears down there. I thought it was worth it."

"It was. I owe you."

"I used what I had on hand of yours. It'll all balance out in the end."

She nodded at the shoulder bag. "What about that?"

He exhaled. "I don't know. I could put it in a safe here, keep it for you."

She shook her head. "I need it liquid. With a fast turnover. I'll be living off it."

"Normally, I'd take it, make an investment in one of our construction projects. Like the deal we had in Alabama with the strip mall. But I don't know if that's a good idea right now. To be honest, having those cops poking around this office, making noises about ethics committees . . . It put the fear of God into me."

"I can see that."

"I don't know what to tell you."

"Maybe you know somebody who knows somebody," she said. "Even if you can't vouch for them."

"This isn't good," he said. "This is no way to do business."

"I need your help."

He sighed, looked at her. Horns sounded in the street below.

"This is where I get nervous," he said. "I have one or two clients like yourself, with special needs. But there are other attorneys who build practices around that, if you know what I mean."

"And you know some of these others?"

"Know, but don't associate with. Don't need to, generally, and don't want to. Occasionally our paths cross, but I try to avoid them as much as possible. Way I look at it, they're begging to be disbarred or worse."

"I don't have any contacts up here anymore, besides you. Otherwise, I'd work it out myself. But with Hector gone . . ."

He chewed a lip. "I still think you should lie low, stash that for a while."

"I can't. I need to move it."

He took a pen from an inside pocket, tapped it on the table, then pulled the legal pad closer. He wrote on it quickly, tore a half page off.

"Here's a name," he said. "He's in Manhattan. I'm not sure of the number." He slid the paper across to her.

"I'll find it." She took the sheet. "He know you?"

"Maybe. But don't use my name. I don't want anything to do with that guy. He may want credentials, contacts of people you've dealt with. I don't know what to tell you about that."

"I'll handle it."

"But I want you to know, I'm not comfortable with this."

"Understood."

"You have a place to stay?"

"I will."

"In the city?"

"No. Close by, though."

"Keep out of Connecticut."

He stood, put out his hand. She took it.

"I'll call you if I hear anything else," he said. "You should put that somewhere safe in the meantime."

"Having second thoughts? That's a lot of money."

He smiled, shook his head.

"And that," he said, "is exactly what I'm worried about."

# SIX

Outside Harrisburg, Benny found a pay phone at a gas station, got change from the clerk inside. He'd never owned a cell phone, was always worried someone could use it to track him down, though he didn't even know if that was possible.

He pumped quarters into the phone, looked across the lot to where the Hyundai was parked. Marta brushing her hair in the rearview. It was noon, and she'd slept most of the way, curled against him. His shoulder was still warm. As he dialed, she turned her head, caught him watching her, gave him a smile.

On the fifth ring, a man answered. "Galaxy."

"Can I speak with Leo?"

"Leo? There's no Leo here."

"I'm trying to reach Leo Bloomgold, the manager there."

"I think you got the wrong place."

"This the Galaxy Lounge in Ozone Park?" He'd gotten the number from information, but was worried now it was the wrong one, a different bar with the same name.

"Yeah," the man said, "but I don't know no Leo."

"This the Galaxy on Lefferts Boulevard, near the airport?"

"Last time I looked, yeah."

"Who's the manager there now? Who's running the joint?"

"Who wants to know?"

Benny sighed. This would be harder than he thought. Realizing again how long he'd been away.

"So you don't know Leo Bloomgold?"

"Do I stutter?"

"He used to run the Golddigger out in Forest Hills, too. You know the place?"

"Never heard of it. Who is this again?"

Benny thumbed the hook switch, listened to coins drop. He looked at his watch. Maybe three more hours before they crossed into Jersey. They'd find someplace to eat around here, then he'd make more calls.

He looked at the traffic rushing by, thought about Rick, probably calling the house right now, wondering where he was. Would he call the police at some point? And Taliferro and the others, where were they now? Had they taken Dominic to a hospital, or left a dead man in his house?

He felt a sudden anger, wanted to smash the receiver against the phone. More than thirty years later, and Joey Dio was still fucking him, only this time from beyond the grave.

He hung up the receiver, forced a smile as he walked back toward the car. Marta leaned over and opened the door for him. She'd tied her hair back in a blue bow. By the time he reached the car, his smile was real.

Look at this, he thought. Sixty-two years old, married and divorced, almost dead more times than he could count, and in love again after all this time. What a world.

\* \* \*

It was dark by the time they reached Staten Island. Benny pulled into the first motel they saw, checked in as Leonard Spiegel, the name on his Indiana driver's license and Visa card.

When they were settled in the room, he went out and used the pay phone by the office, a finger in his ear to block out the clank and hum of the vending machines. He used up the rest of his change making calls.

When he returned to the room, Marta was stretched out on the bed, watching TV. She looked at him, picked up the remote, muted the sound.

"Well?" she said.

He slumped down beside her, looked at the screen. "What's this?"

"It's that show I like, where people send in their videos."

"Oh."

"Are you going to tell me what happened?"

He felt it all catching up with him then—the stress, the hours of driving. His back was stiff, his neck sore.

"We should go get some dinner," he said. "Before I fall asleep."

"What are we going to do?"

"Get a good night's rest, then tomorrow we'll go out, buy whatever things you need. Later on, I have to see someone."

"Who?"

"My brother-in-law."

"I didn't know you had one."

"Technically, I don't. Not anymore."

"Where is he?"

"Bay Ridge."

"Where's that?"

"Brooklyn. It's not far from here. Just over the bridge."

"Is it safe to go there?"

He shrugged. "I guess I'm going to find out."

"Now this," Hersh said, "I don't believe."

They were in the back room of the dry cleaning shop, the door closed, the place reeking of chemicals and mothballs. Benny had to move a pile of plastic hangers from a chair before he could sit.

Hersh sat behind his desk. He wore a crisp white shirt with no tie, suspenders, a thin black and gray sweater, unbuttoned. The desktop was covered with papers, pink receipt slips, a brown-bag lunch spread out over the blotter. Benny could smell tuna fish.

"That was a phone call I never thought I'd get," Hersh said.

"It's good to see you, too." There was a chime as someone came into the front part of the store, where Lily, Hersh's Korean clerk, was behind the counter. "How are you feeling, Hersh?"

"What's that mean?"

"Your health. How are you doing?"

"You mean the diabetes? I'll probably be blind in two years, but what do you care? And what's with you? You look like shit."

"I've had a rough couple days."

"So?"

"Give me a break, Hersh. This isn't easy for me. I wouldn't have called if I didn't need your help. You know that."

"And I should help you why? You show up here out of nowhere, no one's heard from you in, what, twenty-five years? You waltz in here like nothing's changed?"

"A lot has changed," Benny said. He took his glasses off, adjusted the frames, put them back on. They were still off center.

"So, what do you have to say for yourself?" Hersh said.

"First of all, I know you're still angry at me."

"You think so?"

"I'm sorry I wasn't at Rachel's funeral. I wanted to be, but they wouldn't let me. They said it wasn't safe."

"Whatever. No big deal. She was only your wife, right?"

"I loved that woman, Hersh. She was everything to me."

"Until you didn't need her anymore."

"It was her choice to leave. She couldn't take the way we were living anymore. I understand that."

"On the run, at her age? No family, no friends? No wonder she got sick."

"She wasn't sick when she left, Hersh. Or if she was, she didn't tell me. That came later."

"What does that mean? You blame her for leaving? For getting sick?"

"That's not what I said."

"It sounds like it."

"Have you heard from Lena or Ethan? Do they keep in touch?"

Hersh sighed, scratched his elbow. "Benny, I don't know what to tell you."

"They've got a right to hate me. I just need to know they're okay."

"They're fine. They're adults. They've got their own lives."

"Are they out here?"

Hersh didn't answer.

"If you talk to them . . ."

"Benny, I've seen them once or twice the last three years, honest. They're far away from here, both of them."

"They in school?"

"Ethan is. Lena's married."

"Kids?"

"One. A boy."

"So I'm a grandfather."

Hersh shrugged.

"They don't want to see me," Benny said. "I understand that. But if they ever change their minds. . . ."

"Benny, what do you expect me to say?"

"Ten years is a long time, Hersh."

"And three years since Rachel died. Have you ever once visited her grave?"

"I'm sorry. I haven't exactly been free to go where I please. You have no idea what it was like, the life we were leading. Out there in the middle of nowhere, not knowing anybody. You have no right to criticize."

"No, I'm only her brother. What right do I have? Why did you call me?"

"Something came up out there, where I was," Benny said. "I had to leave."

"What's that mean, 'Something came up'?"

"Some guys showed up looking for me. There was trouble."

"What about those people who were protecting you? The FBI, the Sheriff's Department . . ."

"Marshals Service."

"Whatever. What about them?"

"Things didn't work out with that."

"How so?"

"I couldn't live that life anymore, Hersh. Getting dragged all over the country, one trial after another. I left the program."

"Left or got kicked out?"

"Does it matter?"

"So it's kicked out. You're a born fuckup, you know that? Everything you've had in life, you've fucked up."

"Don't start."

"You had your life here, with your Italian friends. Mister Hotshot Gambler, fancy suits, playing the horses, taking bets, fixing basketball games. Top of the world, right? And you fucked that up. Then you had to leave, let the government take care of you, and you fucked that up, too. You had a beautiful wife, two great kids. What happened with that?"

"Yeah, I fucked up. I know that. But things are different now." He thought about Marta back at the motel, watching TV, waiting for him to come home.

"Why?" Hersh said. "You suddenly get a vision? Wisdom come to you in old age?"

"We're not getting anywhere like this."

"I'm sorry. Go ahead, speak your piece."

"These men that came looking for me, they were from Patsy Spinnell's old crew, that worked for Joey Dio."

Hersh frowned. "Patsy's been dead six, seven years. Maybe longer. Joey Dio's gone now, too."

"I heard. Patsy's people are still around, though. Danny Taliferro and a couple of his whyos tracked me down."

"That son of a bitch. How'd they find you?"

"I don't know. I was hoping you might."

Hersh shook his head. "Even if I'd known, I wouldn't have told them. Not out of love for you, but I wouldn't piss on Danny Taliferro if he was on fire. I had to put up with those guys for years, with their hands in everyone's pockets."

"You know what's going on, though. You hear word on the street, right? I mean, Brooklyn's still Brooklyn."

"What are you asking me?"

"Taliferro kept talking about Joey. About the Lufthansa money."

"You'd know more about that than me."

"Bullshit. I never saw a cent of it. And I almost got whacked over it anyway."

"You were Jimmy's friend."

"The Gent didn't have friends."

"So, you were what, his half-Jew mascot?"

"Jimmy got greedy. Joe too. They figured it was easier, cheaper to take people out than pay them. I was next on the hit parade. That's why I went away."

"What you get for messing around with Italians and *schvartzes*. No loyalty. It's all about the money. Jimmy's another one the world won't miss."

"Taliferro said word on the street was that Joey Dio squirreled away his share of the Lufthansa money. Never touched it."

"Maybe. Or maybe it's just an urban legend. Brooklyn's full of them."

"He said now with Joey gone, people might start looking for it. He wanted me to help him. That's why he tracked me down."

"He come heavy?"

Benny nodded.

"How'd you get away?"

"It wasn't easy. I left them out there, but they'll be back."

"Then why are you here, of all places?"

"I need to find out if anyone else is looking for me. What the layout is these days. Who my friends are."

Hersh laced fingers over his stomach, pushed away a little from the desk, chair wheels squeaking. He looked at Benny in silence.

"What?" Benny said.

"You been away a long time."

"We've been over that."

"Things have changed. No one who wanted you dead is even around anymore. Joey Dio was the last one, and he's gone now, too. But there's no crews anymore, not the way there were."

"Hard to feature that."

"There's still plenty of wiseguys around, sure. But when the bosses kept getting sent away, the whole thing fell apart. It just . . . What's the word? 'Devolved.' It's just gangs now. Nickel-and-dime stuff. Gambling, loan sharks, all that, that'll always be around. But the way it used to be? Organized, a chain of command and all that? That's all gone. Everyone's on their own now."

"I called the Galaxy, tried to reach Leo Bloomgold. Didn't have any luck."

"Try a Ouija board."

"What's that mean?"

"Heart attack. Last year, down in Boca. That's where he was living. It's a different world here now, Benny. You could walk down Lefferts Boulevard with a sign that said, I RATTED OUT JIMMY THE GENT and no one would give a shit."

Benny thought that over. Jimmy, Patsy, Joey, and now Leo. All of them gone.

"I thought you'd be happy to hear all this," Hersh said. "You know, almost ten years now, I've been running this business, haven't had to pay a dime protection to anyone? And no-show jobs? At one point, when I had the big shop up on Pelham Parkway, half my staff were gonifs I never even met. Someone would come by every week, pick up their checks. You think I miss that?"

"Is there anyone else around I would know?"

Hersh gave that a moment, shook his head. "Not that I can think of."

"What about over in Jersey?"

"Those were your friends, not mine."

"Jimmy Peaches?"

"Jimmy Falcone? Yeah, I think he's still around. Not doing so well, though, from what I hear. He's down in some retirement place on the Shore."

"Jimmy Junior?"

"In Marion, last I heard. Not coming home."

Benny nodded, stood. "I'll be around for a little bit. Couple, three days at least. Is it okay if I call you again?"

"Why?"

"So we can stay in touch."

"And I can tell you if I hear anything? If anyone comes around asking about you? That the idea?"

"That, too."

"If I did tell you," Hersh said, "it would be because I don't want those kids to be orphans, that's all. It wouldn't be about you."

"I understand." Benny put out his hand.

Hersh looked at it, then at Benny's eyes. Benny left his hand out. After a moment, Hersh sat forward, reached up, shook it.

"I'm sorry," Benny said. "For everything."

When Benny was at the door, Hersh said, "Do you?"

Benny turned. "What?"

"Know where Joey Dio stashed his money?"

"No. Why would I? He was no friend of mine."

"You wouldn't tell me if you did, would you?"

"Forget it, Hersh. Like you said, it was a long time ago."

Marta stayed in the car. He walked along the damp grass, following the directions the caretaker had given, reading the headstones set flush in the ground. They seemed to go on forever.

To his right, behind a high, ivy-choked iron fence, was the steady drone of traffic on the Long Island Expressway. The air smelled of exhaust.

It took him ten minutes to find her. It was a simple granite headstone, the grass overgrown around it. RACHEL ROTH, NEE BRONFMAN, LOVING MOTHER 1949–2009. Someone had left two small stones on the marker. Hersh maybe, or the kids, Hersh lying about where they were.

He knelt, set down the bouquet of yellow roses he'd brought. Her favorite. He tugged at some of the grass around the headstone, tossed it away. The wind took it.

Years ago, when Rachel had first suggested buying plots, he'd refused. It wasn't something he wanted to think about. So this one had been bought after she'd left him, by her or Hersh maybe, when the end seemed near. But it was a single plot. There was no room for him, in the ground or on the headstone.

He stood, his bad knee aching, wiped wet dirt from his pants. I'm sorry, girl, he thought. You were too good for me, always were. Why you put up with me so long, I don't know.

He couldn't remember the last time they'd spoken. The day she'd left, he'd been too drunk or stoned—he wasn't even sure which—to process it. He'd come home late to a silent house, a note on the kitchen table. In a haze, he'd walked the empty rooms, looking for signs of them. Then he'd gone out and sat on the front steps in the cold, looked up at the starry sky over the cornfields, too numb to feel much of anything.

He found a flat stone near the fence, carried it back. He tucked the roses against the side of the marker, laid the stone atop it.

Finally got the chance to say good-bye, honey, he thought. Sorry it took so long.

The wind blowing around him, he limped back to the car.

* * *

Driving back to the motel, Marta said, "We shouldn't stay out here."

"What do you mean?"

"It's not good for you being here, getting mixed up in all this again. We should go somewhere. Florida, maybe. California. Someplace you've never been, where nobody knows you."

Light rain was spotting the windshield. He turned the wipers on.

"Angel, I don't have enough money to get us anywhere. Not to live, anyway."

"You can get a job again, cooking. I can always waitress. God knows I did it long enough. We'll make it work."

"We will. Soon. There's something else I need to look into first."

"What? What's more important than you and me?"

"Those guys in Indiana," he said. "They were after me because of some money that was hidden away a long time ago. A lot of money. They thought I knew where it was."

"Another reason we shouldn't be here."

"Well, that's the thing . . ."

"What?"

"The money. Knowing where it is."

"What about it?"

"I think I do."

# SEVEN

She didn't like it. Here was this big BMW, smoked windows, rims, cruising up Lexington Avenue in the middle of the afternoon, slowing as the driver looked for her. She was where she was supposed to be, the corner of Sixtieth, but now she was getting nervous. It all felt too exposed, too open.

She wore thin black leather gloves. In her left hand was the cup of coffee she'd gotten from a street cart. In her right was the .32, deep in her coat pocket.

The BMW steered to the curb, rear window powering down. The man inside gestured to her.

She sipped coffee, looked up and down the street. Lots of people, but no one watching her. The rear door opened. She dropped her cup in a trash basket, stepped off the curb, got in.

New car smell, shiny leather. As she shut the door, the driver pulled back into traffic. The window slid up silently, the doors locked with a click.

Cavanaugh was in his midthirties. Hair cut short, neatly

trimmed soul patch. He wore a black leather duster over a white shirt, a skinny black tie. He slid over to give her room. His cologne was musky, strong.

"I thought that was you," he said. "But the description you gave was a little off. You're much more attractive in person."

She let that pass. "This car a good idea?"

"Better we talk here than the office. Carlita, my secretary, gets a little nosy. Jealous, too. I'd get rid of her, but she has other talents."

The driver laughed. She looked at him. He was big, Hispanic. She could see tattoos on the fingers of his right hand as he drove—a crucifix, ace of spades. On the back of his wrist, the letters ms in gothic script.

"Romero," Cavanaugh said. "Let's go uptown. Take your time."

To her, he said, "It's Lisa, right?" That was the name she'd given him on the phone. "Good enough for purposes of conversation, I guess. I won't ask your last name. That was too bad about Hector Suarez. I heard what happened. How long did you know him?"

When they'd first spoken, he'd wanted a contact, someone she'd known. She given him Hector's name, but then regretted it. It had felt like a betrayal.

"Long enough."

"Our paths crossed every once in a while, but he never mentioned you. You're a pleasant surprise."

"I made a mistake," she said. Then to the driver, "Pull over here. I'm getting out."

"Hold on," Cavanaugh said. "Romero, keep going, it's all right." He turned to her. "Sorry. But hey, we don't really know each other. You can't blame me for trying to sound you out a little. How do I know you're not a law enforcement officer?"

"I could ask the same."

"Fair enough." They turned into Central Park on the transverse road, Romero watching her in the rearview.

"So, let's talk," Cavanaugh said. "You implied you had some funds you're looking to invest, short term."

"That's right."

"How much are we talking about?"

"Six figures."

"Low six or high?"

"Low."

He thumbed his soul patch. "This isn't my main line of the work, you know. I just do it as a sideline sometimes, for friends."

"We're not friends."

"No, but that could change. How temporary an investment are we talking about?"

"Short as possible. I need a quick turnover."

"That's always a problem. It'll affect the exchange rate."

She didn't respond. She was liking it less every minute.

"What's the heat level?" he said.

"Bills are untraceable for the most part. Unsequenced. But the majority of them are new."

"Acquired where?"

"Does that matter?"

"If it was around here, it does."

"It wasn't."

"Denominations?"

"Twenties mostly. Some tens."

"If the heat's low, why exchange them?"

"I like to be careful."

They'd come out on the other side of the park. Romero got on the West Side Highway north. They passed the Ninety-sixth Street exit, and she thought about her apartment at 108th and Broadway, where she'd lived as Roberta Summersfield only four months ago. It felt like years.

"As I said, this isn't my main line. And even though I believe everything you're saying, I can't be certain, you know? There might be an issue with the money you're not telling me."

"There isn't."

"And a rush job, too. It increases my risk, because—"

"Name the rate."

He stroked his chin again. They passed Grant's Tomb, the George Washington Bridge looming in the distance.

"Well," he said. "Quick turnaround, that amount, I'd say ten cents on the dollar. That's all I could give you."

"Forget it."

"You think you can get a better deal, go find it."

"For ten cents on a dollar, I'll take my chance with the bills."

"You could do that." He looked out the window.

"You'll come out way ahead on this however it goes," she said. "You know that. Fifty and we keep talking."

"Fifty?" He looked back at her. "Forget that. No way I could do fifty in that time frame. Wouldn't if I could. Twenty, and that's generous."

"Then we'll say thirty."

"I can do it quick, if that's what you need. But not for more than twenty-five."

Twenty-five cents on the dollar. That would be thirty-seven thousand to her, free and clear. Less than she wanted, but enough to stake her.

"That could work," she said.

"Good. I can make the deal even better for you, though. A lot better."

"How's that?"

"Let's say I give you half in cash, half in something you can sell yourself. You could double, triple your money."

"No, thanks."

"Don't dismiss the idea so quick."

"Twenty-five on the dollar," she said. "I've got a hundred and fifty on hand, that means thirty-seven five back to me."

"You're quick with the math."

"I'll need the money by the end of this week."

"You're kidding, right?"

"No." She looked at him. "Part of the deal."

"I don't know if I can swing that."

"You'll figure it out."

To the driver, she said, "Take this exit. There's a subway stop at Broadway and One-fifty-seventh. Drop me there."

"You're a tough bargainer," Cavanaugh said. "You want everything on your own terms, don't you?"

"We already named the price. I'm taking a seventy-five percent loss. That's more than I ever would normally. You want to go through with it, or not?"

Romero turned down the exit ramp, stopped at a light.

"You put it that way, I've got no choice," Cavanaugh said. He touched her leg. "You should think on that other offer, though. Trust me, it could be very lucrative for you."

She looked at his hand. He took it away.

"Thanks, anyway," she said. "But like you said, not my line."

They turned right and headed back down Broadway, 157th coming up. Romero looked into the rearview. Cavanaugh nodded. The BMW pulled to the curb. Cars sounded their horns, veered around them.

Cavanaugh put out his hand. Crissa looked at it. When he didn't pull it back, she let go of the .32, shook his hand. She left the glove on.

"A deal, then," he said. "Mutually beneficial, I hope."

"I'll get the bills together. Then we can pick a place to meet. Somewhere outside the city."

She opened the door, started to get out.

"Wait a minute," he said. "How do I get in touch with you?"

She stepped onto the sidewalk.

"You don't," she said. "I'll call you."

She shut the door.


Belmar was a summer town, the tourists long gone now. From the window of her motel room, she could see a long stretch of empty boardwalk, gray waves pounding the desolate beach. She called Rathka.

It was almost five, but Monique answered on the second ring. When Rathka came on the line, Crissa said, "I don't like him."

"I warned you. Normally, I wouldn't let somebody like that within a hundred miles of you. But you said—"

"I know. I'm not blaming you. But he makes me nervous. He acts like a wannabe. And his driver's a gangbanger, or at least was. MS-13. Salvadoran."

"I wouldn't know anything about that. But if you don't like the way it feels, walk away."

"Not sure I can this time. How well do you know Cavanaugh?"

"Not very. Can you make it work?"

"Maybe," she said. "Anything new from Texas?"

"Not yet. I'm hoping for an update soon. Are you okay? Do you need anything?"

"A place to live. I'm in New Jersey, at a motel, but I want something else. A house, condo maybe."

"Where?"

"Down at the Shore. It's good here now. No one around. I'll sign a lease if necessary. I can do a cashier's check for the security."

"I'll find something. So, you're going to go through with this other thing?"

"I have to," she said. "I have no choice."

The money was in a brown paper shopping bag with a reinforced bottom and sturdy twine handles. She'd laid a cheap T-shirt over the top, kept the bag between her feet, half hidden beneath the park bench.

She was looking out over New York Harbor, the Statue of Liberty. This stretch of Jersey City along the river had been turned into a park. There were benches and bike paths, a flagstone promenade. Across the Hudson, the late-afternoon sun lit the Manhattan skyline, flashing off skyscraper glass. There were whitecaps on the water, a stiff wind pushing them along. A loose sheet of newspaper blew past her feet.

She knotted her scarf tighter, zipped up her jacket. She was alone in the park. Out in the shipping lanes, she could see a freighter making its way into the harbor, a city block's worth of containers lined up on its deck.

She heard a car, looked behind her to see the BMW pull into one of the diagonal spaces. Her Fusion was parked a few spots away. There were no other cars in the lot.

She looked back over the water. Gulls squawked above her. Two of them landed, strutted around an overfilled trash can, picking through bits of garbage on the ground.

She tightened her grip on the .32 in her pocket, heard a car door open and close. Romero came around the bench. He wore a belted trench coat, hands in his pockets.

"Cold," he said. He sat beside her.

"I want news by the day after tomorrow," she said. "Friday at the latest."

"Four days? You like to push it, don't you?"

"Friday or we've got a problem."

"That a threat?"

"No." She stood up. "Just the way it is. I'll call him tomorrow, see where we are."

"Whatever." He was looking across the river. "Nice view."

"Enjoy it."

At the car, she looked back, saw he'd pulled the bag closer. He picked up the T-shirt, looked in, then covered the money again.

She got in, started the engine. He stayed where he was, looking out at the harbor. He didn't turn when she drove past.

# EIGHT

The next day, she made the ten-minute drive from Belmar to Asbury Park. The retirement home was twenty stories of concrete facing an empty stretch of boardwalk, the beach beyond. The wind was coming in strong off the ocean, blowing spray from the top of the waves.

She parked in the lot, took the gift-wrapped package from the seat beside her, got out. Near the entrance, wind whipped an American flag high on a pole.

A visitor's pass from the main desk, then an elevator ride to the tenth floor. The corridor smelled of disinfectant and floor wax. She could hear someone crying softly behind a door at the opposite end.

She walked past half-open doors, low TV sounds coming from within. Through one doorway, she saw an ancient white-haired woman propped up in bed, skeletal hands folded on the sheet in front of her. She stared at Crissa as she went past.

That might be you someday, Crissa thought. If you live that long.

Jimmy Peaches's room was at the end of the hall, the door ajar. She knocked, looked in to see a man leaning against a dresser, arms folded. He was in his thirties, dark, muscular, wearing a polo shirt, jeans. He nodded at her, said, "Come in." Then, "*Nonno*, your date's here."

When she came in, Jimmy was seated beside the bed. It took her a moment to realize he was in a wheelchair.

He smiled when he saw her. "There you are. Let me look at you."

"Jimmy," she said. "*Come sta?*"

He stirred as if to get up, then stayed where he was. He looked frailer than the last time she'd seen him, but immaculate as always. Buttoned-down pale blue shirt with the monogram JCF, yellow slacks, shiny black shoes. But his white hair, combed straight back, was thinner, and she could see patches of pink scalp. His bony arms seemed lost in the shirtsleeves.

He raised his hands, let them fall. "Forgive me for being rude. First time in my life I haven't been able to stand to greet a lady."

"It's okay, Jimmy," she said. "Stay where you are." She set the package on the bed, took one of his hands. He squeezed, but there was little behind it.

"I've been worried about you since the last time we talked," he said. "It's good to see you. Anthony, get her a chair."

Anthony took a hard plastic chair from a desk, brought it near the bed. The room was smaller than she'd expected, with only a couch, a table, and a flat-screen television. Railings on the sides of the bed, the left one unlocked and hanging down. A walker folded shut and leaning against the wall.

She pulled the chair closer, sat. "How are you, Jimmy?"

He shrugged. "You can see. Not so good. But I guess it's all relative, right? I'm alive. This is my grandson, Anthony Falcone. You've heard me talk about him maybe."

She looked at Anthony, nodded.

He said, "All good stuff, I hope."

She gestured at the big window facing the ocean. "I see you've got the best room, as always. You still running the place?"

"He practically does," Anthony said.

"They moved me up here last month. I used to be down a couple floors. Bigger room, much nicer. Then I had my fall."

"What happened?"

"Ah, it's not even worth talking about."

"Tell her," Anthony said.

"It was stupid. Coming out of the bathroom. Slipped, I guess, went down. I couldn't even tell you how. Woke up on the floor."

"You hurt yourself?"

"A little."

"Broken hip," Anthony said.

"I'm sorry," she said.

Jimmy shrugged. "Like I said, stupid. All my fault. My age, though, they don't like to operate. So I've got the therapy three times a week, and maybe someday, if I'm lucky, I'm back on the walker and out of this chair."

"You'll get there," Anthony said. "You just gotta do what they tell you."

"Whatever," Jimmy said. He looked at the package. "That for me?"

"Yes. Although now I'm having second thoughts."

"I'll be the judge of that. Let's have a look."

She handed him the package. It was wrapped in simple green paper, tied with string. He had trouble working the knot, the knuckles of both hands knobby and bent. She started to help, but Anthony shook his head. She sat back.

Jimmy got the knot untied, undid the tape, peeled back the paper to reveal the ornate white and gold box beneath.

"Portofinos," he said. "Nice. Thank you."

"The last time I was here, you said you hadn't had a cigar in a long time, couldn't afford them."

"He exaggerates," Anthony said.

Jimmy fingered the broken seal on the box. She'd closed it with tape. "You try one of these yourself?"

"No. I put a little something extra in there. It's not much. I owe you more, for all your help last time."

Anthony went to the door, shut it.

"You don't owe me anything," Jimmy said.

"I feel I do. But should you be smoking these days?"

"I'll have Anthony sneak me out. Take a stroll on the boardwalk when the weather's nicer. Time was, I could light one up in the sunroom out front. Staff would look the other way. These days, forget about it."

He undid the tape, opened the box. It was full, twenty-five cigars in thin metal tubes.

"They're a little more high-end than normal," she said.

"Are they?" He unscrewed one of the tubes, saw the edge of the bills with the cigar tucked in the center. She'd put two hundreds in each tube, five thousand dollars in all. It was money from her original stake, nothing from the ATMs.

"Very generous," he said.

"Least I could do."

He closed the tube, replaced it in the box. "I'm glad you're doing well. I was worried about that other thing. I saw some of it in the papers."

When she didn't respond, he said, "We can talk freely. Anthony knows all my business. But he'll leave if you want him to."

"Up to you," Anthony said to her. "Either way's fine with me."

"No, that's okay," she said. "Stay."

"I told him a little about you," Jimmy said. "He can be over-protective sometimes. I only gave him as much as he needed to know, of course. Nothing past that."

"Thanks a lot," Anthony said.

"It's all right," she said. "I understand."

She'd never met Anthony's father, Jimmy Junior, but knew he was in federal prison in Illinois, a long bid on a RICO case. As far as she knew, Anthony was Jimmy's only grandchild.

"So," Jimmy said. He set the box and loose paper on the bed. "What are you doing these days?"

"Was down south for a while. Back up here now, trying to get some things together. I've got a line on a place nearby, maybe moving in tomorrow."

"How'd that thing last year play out?"

"It cost me. Money. Resources. But I think it's done. No more blowback. No long-standing consequences."

"Good. And our friend in Texas?"

Back in the '90s, when she and Wayne had worked the North-east, Jimmy had steered them to a long string of high-dollar scores. Then Wayne had gone to Houston with a three-man crew on what was supposed to be a give-up job at a jewelry wholesaler. It had gone bad fast. Wayne took a bullet in the shoulder, and their driver wiped out during the getaway, put himself through the windshield and both of them into prison. The third man, a pro named Larry Black, had gotten away.

"There's a hearing at the end of this month," she said. "We'll see what happens."

"How are his chances?"

"Good, I think. I've tried to help pave the way, spread some cash around down there. I'm hoping it'll pay off."

"Lawyers, judges," Jimmy said. "You can never trust them, even when you're filling their pockets. They get an idea there's some sort of principle involved, then they turn around and fuck you anyway, keep your money. Excuse my French."

"Let's hope that's not the case."

"I'm sorry. I don't mean to be negative. If you talk to him, see him, give him my best."

"I will. Can't do it right now, though. That trouble up here, it dead-ended a couple things for me. I need to start over, get a stake together."

"How are you set right now?"

"Got a little cash saved up. Enough to pay the bills. There's some more I'm trying to turn over quickly. I'll have to take a hit on it, but there's not much I can do."

"Who's handling it?"

"Friend of a friend. Don't know him, but there wasn't time to shop around."

"Be careful."

"If that doesn't work out," Anthony said, "let me know. Maybe I can help."

"Listen to him," Jimmy said. "Mister Kingpin."

"I'm just saying." He looked at Crissa. "I run a restaurant. Handle a lot of cash."

"Thanks," she said. "But I'll be fine."

"Don't get the wrong impression," Jimmy said. "Anthony likes to talk like he's Nicky Newark sometimes, but he isn't. He went to business school at Rutgers. He's got a good head on his shoulders. He's just lucky no one's knocked it off."

"Just making the offer," Anthony said.

"I'll keep it in mind." She touched Jimmy's hand. "I need to get going, but I'll try to come back soon. Maybe later this week. Anything I can bring you?"

He nodded at the box. "You've done more than enough already."

"It's a gesture, that's all. I'll give Anthony my cell number. It'll be good for a while. If you need anything, call. When it changes, I'll get the new one to you as well." She stood.

*"Grazie,"* he said. "Anthony, get the door for the lady."

"I got it, *nonno.*" He took a suitcoat from the back of a chair. "I'll walk you out."

She took Jimmy's hand in both of hers, felt the birdlike bones beneath the skin. "Take care of yourself, Jimmy. I'll be in touch."

He squeezed weakly. *"Statti bene."*

At the elevator, Anthony said, "I appreciate your coming by like this. It means a lot to him."

"We go back. How's he doing, really? I know you couldn't talk much in there."

"He's eighty-two, what can you say? Every time something happens, it takes him longer to recover. He's a fighter, though. Hope I'm half as strong at that age. Whether he's going to walk again or not, that's another question."

"I'm sorry." They got on the elevator.

"Right after the fall, he wasn't doing so good," he said. "I thought we were gonna lose him for a while. But he's been coming along slowly. He perked right up when you called. He was looking forward to seeing you."

In the lobby they returned their visitor's passes, walked out into the wind. There were only a half dozen cars in the parking lot.

He nodded at the Ford. "That your ride?"

"For now. It's a rental. You don't live around here, I take it?"

"Nah." He got a pack of cigarettes from his coat pocket, dealt one out, offered it to her. She shook her head. "I'm up in Nutley, but I'm down here two, three times a week now." He took out a lighter, got the cigarette going after two tries, hands cupped against the wind. A metal halyard clattered against the flagpole.

He blew smoke out. "So, you married? I mean, I didn't see a ring or anything."

She almost smiled at that. "No." She got out her keys.

"Engaged? It's none of my business, I'm just asking."

"Sort of."

"The guy down in Texas, one my grandfather was asking about?"

"That's the one."

"Too bad. That he's inside, I mean."

"It is."

"Don't get me wrong," he said. "I didn't mean anything by that."

"Don't worry about it. How about you?"

"Married? No. Used to be. Not anymore."

"Sorry to hear that."

"Way it goes. Listen, I heard what you said and all, but maybe we can have a drink or something sometime, you know? Just talk."

"Maybe," she said. She unlocked the car. "Look after your grandfather. He's a good man."

"I will."

When she pulled out, she looked in the rearview, saw he was still standing there in the wind, watching her drive away.

# NINE

The place Rathka found for her was on the inlet in Avon, just north of Belmar. It was a one-story, single-family house, the backyard sloping down to the water and a small dock. A sliding glass door in the living room gave onto a back deck. From there, she could see where the inlet emptied into the ocean, a quarter mile away.

The other houses on the street were summer rentals, empty now. She'd paid three months in advance for this one, $1,500 a month and security, no lease. The house was furnished, but hadn't been lived in for months.

She'd driven the Focus long enough, never liked to keep the same car for long. She'd returned it at a local office, then taken a cab to another rental company a few miles away. She'd driven out with a Ford Taurus, stopped for groceries and wine on the way home.

There was a wall unit in the living room, TV and stereo. She searched the dial until she found WQXR, the classical station out of New York. It was almost all she'd listened to when she'd lived there.

The Tomcat lay disassembled on a sheet of newspaper on the kitchen table. She cleaned and oiled it with a kit she'd bought at a sporting goods store. The magazine held seven rounds. She unloaded it, tested the spring, then thumbed the shells back in. Handel's "Sarabande" filled the empty rooms.

When the gun was reassembled, she wiped it down with a rag, then fit the magazine into the grip until it seated. She worked the slide to test the action, and chamber a round. It wasn't much of a weapon, but it would have to do. She lowered the hammer, slipped the safety on, set the gun atop the refrigerator.

The wine was a Chateau d'Arcins, Haut-Medoc. She opened it to let it breathe, then found a dusty wineglass in a kitchen cabinet. She rinsed it out, turned the radio louder, carried glass and bottle out onto the deck.

Chill out here, but the wind felt good, brought the smell of the tide with it. She set the bottle and glass on the wrought-iron table, pulled out the matching chair. The sun was somewhere behind the clouds, fighting to get through.

She left the door open so she could hear the music. Wind riffled the vertical blinds behind her. Water sloshed gently against the dock.

She poured wine, thought about Wayne in a five-by-nine prison cell in Texas, and Jimmy, living out his final years in a retirement home, every day bringing a new indignity, stealing part of the man he used to be.

And what would she do when her own string was played out? If she stayed in the life, the odds were against her. Prison or a bullet. She'd come close to both in December, and only luck had gotten her out of it alive.

She drank wine, looked out at the water, and listened to the wind.

The hotel was on the edge of Newark Airport, planes passing by every few minutes, clawing their way into the sky. She left the Taurus in the short-term lot, walked back to the terminal and got a cab. The Tomcat was in the small of her back, tucked into her belt, her sweater pulled down over it. She wore the leather gloves.

Cavanaugh's suite was on the twelfth floor. They'd agreed on the hotel. It would be better like this, a public place in the middle of the afternoon. Less chance of someone getting stupid.

At the door, she could hear muffled conversation inside. When she knocked, it stopped.

She unzipped her jacket. Footsteps on carpet, and then the door opened.

"*Ola*," Romero said. He stepped aside to let her in, shut the door behind her.

They were in a mirrored foyer. Cavanaugh was in the big room beyond, sitting on a couch, his arms spread over the back. He wore black slacks, a white shirt unbuttoned halfway down his chest. There was a wide window behind him, the curtains pushed back for a view of leaden sky. He was smiling.

"Come on in," he said. "Have a seat."

Romero went past her into the living room, to a sideboard with bottles and glasses. She looked around. There was a hallway to the right, closed doors. Bedroom, bathroom.

"Relax," Cavanaugh said. "Want a drink?"

She shook her head. "No, thanks. Let's just do this, all right?"

"Fair enough."

Romero plinked ice into two square glasses, poured an inch

of scotch into each of them. He set one on the glass coffee table in front of Cavanaugh, sipped the other himself. He wore a suit jacket over an open shirt, polished cowboy boots with silver toe caps.

She heard a toilet flush, turned, right elbow easing back the tail of her jacket. One of the doors opened, and a man came out. A younger version of Romero. Dark-skinned, wiry, hair freshly slicked back. Suit jacket with the sleeves pushed up. Tattoos on his hands and forearms.

She looked at Cavanaugh. "Who's this?"

"That's Jorge. He works for me."

"In your office?"

"Sometimes." Cavanaugh sipped scotch. He gestured to a chair. She moved it to get an angle on the whole room, sat.

Jorge took a seat next to the sideboard. Romero went to the window, swirled scotch in his glass. She heard the rumble of a plane going by overhead.

"So," Cavanaugh said. "You surprised I came through for you?"

"Should I be?" she said.

"Maybe, being as we're practically strangers. But I think you're going to be very happy we met."

"Okay."

"Jorge," he said. "Go ahead, get it for her."

She watched Jorge get up, go back down the hallway, heard a door open. He came out with a leather briefcase, brought it over to Cavanaugh, set it flat on the table.

"What you came for," Cavanaugh said. He set his glass down, swiveled the briefcase so the latches faced him. Jorge went back to his seat.

"Those bills were better than I thought," Cavanaugh said. He opened the briefcase, took out a wide, overstuffed manila envelope. "There've been a lot of phony twenties around, so I was a little wary, you know? But I checked all of them out. They were as good as you said. So, I thought in that case I might do a little better. I made it thirty cents on the dollar."

Forty-five grand to her, instead of thirty-seven. Still not good, but better.

"Thanks," she said. "But you're still coming out way ahead."

"Maybe. But I'm also the one taking the risk."

"The risk was mine, getting those bills in the first place."

"True that. But it's like they say, CREAM, baby."

"What?"

"CREAM—Cash Rules Everything Around Me. You never heard that one?"

She shook her head. With the briefcase open, she couldn't see what else was inside. He set the manila envelope on the table.

"Go ahead," he said. "That's yours."

She looked at Jorge, then Romero. They were watching her, but hadn't moved. She got up from the chair, picked up the envelope, sat back down.

"I think you're going to find doing business with me is a very lucrative proposition," he said.

She frowned at his use of the word again, opened the flimsy clasp. Banded bills inside. She riffled through the packs, then shook them out on her lap. She counted them twice. Twenty thousand.

"Where's the rest?"

He picked up his glass, sipped scotch. "That's just the cash end. Small change compared to what you can have by this time next week."

The window rattled. Another plane going by.

"We had a deal," she said. She put the money back in the envelope.

"And now I'm offering you a better one."

She set the envelope against the chair leg, wanting her hands free. She flexed her fingers inside the gloves. Romero put his glass on the windowsill.

"You know what this is?" Cavanaugh said. He took a bundle the size of a paperback book from the briefcase, set it on the table. Brown paper wrapped in plastic, taped shut.

"I don't want to know," she said. "I just want my money."

"There it is, right there. Twenty-five K worth of the best coke in the Northeast. So pure, you can step on it five, six times, and it'll still blaze. You can turn that into seventy-five thousand easy, maybe more. I can help you do it."

"Are you fucking kidding me?"

His smile disappeared. "Do I look like I'm kidding you?"

"Either that, or you're just stupid. This is bullshit." She stood, the envelope falling over.

"Easy there," Romero said. Jorge leaned forward in his chair.

"You should sit down," Cavanaugh said. "Think about the opportunity I'm offering you."

"I did. And I gave you my answer."

"Your loss." He put the bundle back in the briefcase. "Go ahead, take your money and go."

"You owe me twenty-five thousand."

He shrugged. "I offered you a deal. You turned up your nose at it. Like you said, you made your choice."

She looked at Romero. He'd left the glass where it was, come around the couch to stand on Cavanaugh's left. He'd have a gun beneath the suit jacket. Jorge, too. She had to keep the situation calm, get out of there, then figure out what to do next. But leaving without the rest of the money would sting.

"Well?" Cavanaugh said.

She bent, picked up the envelope.

Jorge was on his feet. He said, "Stop right there, *chica*." Then to the others, "She's carrying."

Cavanaugh frowned. Romero came toward her. She took a step back, and then Jorge had an automatic in his hand. He touched the muzzle to her head.

Romero stood in front of her. She was aware of his size, could smell a faint undercurrent of sweat.

"Belt," Jorge said. "Under the coat."

Romero looked into her eyes. Jorge poked her ear with the gun, a Ruger .380. "Don't move, *puta*. Not a cunt hair."

Romero reached around, patted her hips through the leather, felt the gun. Without taking his eyes off hers, he hiked up the coat. His hand passed across her waist, the tightness of her buttocks. She flinched. He reached up under her sweater, pulled the Tomcat free, stepped back. Cavanaugh stood.

"You come to a meeting with me," he said, "carrying a gun?"

Romero looked over the .32, handed it to him. Cavanaugh ejected the magazine, tossed it onto the couch. He pulled the slide back, saw the round there.

"One in the chamber, huh?" he said. "You fucking bitch."

His right hand came up fast, caught her across the face, snapped her head to the side. Her temple thumped into the muzzle of Jorge's gun.

"What I should do," Cavanaugh said, "is make you suck all of our dicks right here, right now. What do you think about that?"

She looked back at him. "You sure you've got one?"

He slapped her again, brought water to her eyes. She looked past him at Romero. No gun in his hands yet, but he would be the real threat.

Cavanaugh reached out, pinched her left breast hard. She

pulled away. The Ruger touched her head again. Cavanaugh smiled.

"You're lucky I'm in a good mood today," he said. He tossed the Tomcat onto the couch. "Go on. Get out of here. Do it now, before I change my mind."

She looked at him, didn't move. He stepped back. "Go on. Out."

She reached for the envelope. He swept it aside with his foot, money spilling out.

"No," he said. "You had your chance. I offered the deal, you turned me down. *Finito.* Now get out of here."

Jorge stepped away to let her by, lowering his gun.

"I'm giving you ten seconds," Cavanaugh said. "After that, you *can't* leave. You'll be on your knees for all of us. Then Romero will call some of his Salvadoran buddies, and we'll make a real evening of it."

"Go on," Romero said. "He's serious. *Vamos.*"

She backed away, cheek still burning, started for the door. Jorge's gun was at his side. When she passed, he flicked his tongue at her. She stopped, turned to him.

"You like that, *mamacita*?" he said.

She let her expression soften. "Maybe."

"You want some? I'll give you all you can handle."

Romero was frowning. Another plane flew past. The glasses on the sideboard shook.

"That a promise?" she said. He smiled, stepped in closer, and she put a thumb deep into his left eye.

He moved the way she thought he would, whipping his head back, turning to his left, the gun coming up. She slapped her left hand over the barrel, got her right hand on his wrist, twisted, and put her right shoulder hard into his chest. He went back over the chair and into the sideboard, taking down bottles and glasses as he fell. Then she had the Ruger, was coming around with it in her hand.

Cavanaugh froze. Romero started to back away, reaching under his coat. "Don't," she said, and when the gun came out anyway, she shot him through the right shoulder.

Cavanaugh jumped at the noise. The shot blew Romero back, dropped him. She swiveled to cover all of them, the Ruger in a two-handed grip. Cavanaugh stood still.

Romero lay on his side, right hand outstretched, still holding the dark automatic. She brought a boot heel down hard on his wrist, then kicked the gun from his grip, took a step and kicked it again. It slid across the carpet and under the couch.

The noise of the plane died away. Cavanaugh hadn't moved. Jorge was on his knees now, a hand over his eye, breathing hard. The smell of alcohol drifted up from the carpet.

Wayne's voice in her head: *Keep the momentum. Take control of the situation. Don't let it fall apart on you.*

She pointed the Ruger at Cavanaugh's face. "Kneel."

"Listen," he said. "I don't . . ."

She thumbed back the hammer for effect. He looked into her eyes and she knew what he saw there. He raised his hands to shoulder height, lowered himself to his knees.

Romero was trying to sit up, a hand over his shoulder. His eyes fluttered. Slipping into shock, she thought. No exit wound. At that range, the bullet would have punched through tissue, bone and muscle, mushroomed somewhere inside.

She looked at the door, wondered how long it would take before someone came knocking.

Cavanaugh sensed her uncertainty. "What do you think you're going to do?" he said. "Kill us? In here? How far you think you'll get?"

She looked at him, knowing then what she would do, no anger in it. He saw her expression, her shift in balance, tried to pull back out of the way. She took two steps, raised her right foot, drove her boot heel into his face, all her weight behind it. She felt the nose give way, and he went over backward, body limp. He fell onto his side and lay still.

She went to Jorge, pointed the Ruger at his head. When he took his hand away, his left eye was red, already swelling shut. He raised a hand to ward her off.

"Get up," she said. "Keep your hands away from your body."

He got slowly to his feet. "You fucked up my eye."

"Pick up the money," she said.

He did as he was told. Romero was on his back now, eyes closed, but still breathing. She stayed clear of him, watched as Jorge shoveled bills back into the envelope.

"My gun, too," she said. "And the magazine."

"The what?"

"The clip."

He got the Tomcat from the couch.

"In the envelope," she said.

He dropped it in, the magazine after it.

"Put it on the chair," she said. "Then back up, face the wall."

He set the envelope down, raised his left hand back to his eye, didn't move.

"The wall. Or I'll shoot you where you stand."

"I don't think you will, *chica*."

Cavanaugh moaned, trembled. They both looked at him. The carpet around his face was red with blood.

"You're in deep now, *puta*," Jorge said. "That was my brother you shot. You better kill me, too. Because you know we're gonna find you."

"Turn around."

When he did, she decocked the Ruger, reversed it. No easy thing, knocking a man out with a gun. Just as likely to cause brain damage or death. But it couldn't be helped.

"I'm telling you, *chica* . . ." he started, and she stepped forward, brought the butt of the Ruger down in a hard arc. He staggered, reached back to cover his head, but she got the second blow between his hands, drove him forward. With the third he lost his legs, fell against the wall, and slid down into a pile.

Time to move. She stepped around Cavanaugh, turned the briefcase over on the table. The bundle of dope. A .25 automatic with pearl grips. A small mirror and razor blade, to sample the coke if they'd gotten that far. But no more money.

She dropped the .25 into her right coat pocket, pushed the couch aside until she saw Romero's gun, a Smith & Wesson automatic. She put it in the other pocket, felt its weight.

No time to check the rest of the suite. And no use, more than likely. Cavanaugh hadn't come to pay what he'd owed, he'd come to deal.

She put the Ruger in with the .25, tucked the envelope under her arm. She went out into the empty hallway, pockets heavy with guns. The elevator was humming, the display numbers rising: EIGHT, NINE, TEN. The rattle of the car coming up.

She was calmer than she thought she'd be. She took the fire stairs to the eighth floor, went down the hall. Halfway along the corridor was a nook with a soda machine, icemaker, and a white flip-top trash can. She unloaded the .25, dropped it in the bin, did the same with Romero's S&W and the Ruger. She kept the magazines, took an elevator down to the lobby.

There was a police car outside the front door, the rollers on but no one inside. The clerk at the reception desk looked worried. So they'd already gone up. Someone had called in the shot.

She went past the desk, and out into the gray day. There was a shuttle bus waiting at the curb, engine running, people inside. The door started to hiss closed.

She walked fast, stepped off the curb in front of the bus, waved. The tired-looking black man behind the wheel nodded. The door folded open again and she went up, took a seat in the back. As they pulled away, she saw another police car approach, lights flashing. It parked behind the first one.

There were six other people on the bus, but no one made eye contact with her on the five-minute ride to the airport. She thanked the driver, walked to the lot and got her car, headed south on the Turnpike, the envelope with the money and the .32 tucked under her seat.

At the first rest stop she saw, she pulled in, got out her cell and called Rathka. When he came on the line, she said, "You need to be careful."

"What's that mean?"

"That thing with your friend went wrong."

"I knew it. Are you okay?"

"I'm fine. Is there any way they can tie you to me?"

"I don't think so. Christ, I should have talked you out of this."

"Not your fault."

"What happened?"

"He turned out to be triplets. Bad guys. They're down for a while, but it won't be long." Maybe longer, she thought, if no one was awake enough to flush the coke before the police got up there.

"I'm sorry about this," he said. "I feel like I'm to blame."

"You're not. Just the way it went down. I should have listened to my instincts."

"What are you going to do now?"

"What do you mean?"

"How did you leave it? Will they come after you?"

"Not anytime soon," she said.

"What if they do?"

"I'll worry about that when it happens," she said, and ended the call.

She went into the Arby's to use the bathroom, splashed water in her face, looked in the mirror.

Nothing's ever easy, she thought. No matter how much you plan, allow for every contingency. Things go bad, and then you have to work twice as hard just to get back to where you started.

She dried her face with paper towels, went out, pulled the gloves back on. There was a Dumpster near the car. She took out the three magazines, tossed them up and in. She kept the .32.

# TEN

She was in the living room, sleet crackling against the sliding glass door, when Anthony Falcone called.

"I've got bad news for you," he said. "About the money."

She crossed to the stereo, turned the volume down. "Bad news is all I get lately."

"Your hunch was right. I took a close look at all the bills that guy gave you, especially the watermarks and security strips. Ran them under blacklight, too. The tens are all good, but the twenties . . ."

"Tell me."

"More than half are bad. Pretty decent work, though. A lot of these going around lately. I flagged a couple at the restaurant last month."

Another of Cavanaugh's sidelines. And now something else he owed her.

"What's the damage?" she said.

"You could try to float the twenties somewhere, recoup a little of your loss, but I wouldn't recommend it."

"How much in good bills?"

"Ten grand. Maybe."

Ten grand, out of a hundred and fifty. All her work undone, the risk wasted.

"I'm sorry," he said. "I know it's not what you wanted to hear. Bad luck."

More than that, she thought. Bad planning, bad moves. She'd walked right into all of it, like an amateur. And now her stake was down to almost nothing. She rubbed the tattoo on her wrist.

"Appreciate your help," she said.

"Let me know where you want to meet, and I'll turn it all back over to you. I'm guessing you copied the serial numbers beforehand, so you'll know I didn't switch anything out."

"I did. Nothing personal. No offense."

"None taken. If I were you, though, I'd ditch these twenties as soon as possible. They're more trouble than they're worth."

"I will."

"One other thing. I'm not sure what it's about."

"What's that?"

"My grandfather called today. There's someone he wants you to meet."

She frowned. "Who?"

"Don't know. He didn't tell me. But you know my grandfather. If it wasn't important, he wouldn't mention it."

"He give you any idea of the reason?"

"No. I have to call him back after I talk to you. He said if you were willing, he'd set it up. If not, forget about it. No problem. But that I should tell you it might be worth your while."

She knew the phrase. It was the one Jimmy used when he was

steering them to work back in the '90s, a decade's worth of scores with no drama, no blowback. Before the jewelry store in Houston, before everything went to hell.

"Tell him to set it up," she said. "Then call me."

She sat in the hard plastic chair, watching the man a few feet opposite her, not liking what she saw. Late fifties, early sixties. Balding, glasses. Nervous. Jimmy had introduced him as Leonard. He'd taken the chair near the window, sat half-facing her.

Jimmy wheeled into the space between them. The door was closed, Anthony out in the hall to make sure they weren't disturbed.

"Let me just say this first," Jimmy said. "I've known you both a long time. You both have my trust, for what that's worth. And I'll leave it at that."

Leonard fidgeted, looked out the window, then at his watch. Instinct told her to get up, walk out. The circle of people she dealt with was small, and this man was a stranger. But Jimmy had vouched for him. Leaving now would be an insult.

"I don't know about this," Leonard said. He was mumbling, couldn't make eye contact, but she picked up the accent. New York. Brooklyn, maybe. Queens.

"About what?" Jimmy said.

"This place. Talking here. I don't know if it's a good idea."

"It's as good as anywhere," Jimmy said. "I just wanted to make the introduction. You two want to talk more, you can go off somewhere yourselves. If you don't, that's fine, too."

"I don't know," Leonard said again. He took off his glasses, fiddled with the frames, put them back on.

"Whatever," Jimmy said. "We're here now." He looked at

Crissa. "B . . . uh, Leonard here came to me with something of a proposition. Might be up your alley, might not."

"What kind of proposition?"

"Better he tells it. I heard it all, but it's your opinion that matters."

Leonard picked lint off his pants, his right heel rubbed at the carpet. This is more than nerves, she thought. This is fear.

"I'm sorry," he said. "It threw me. I mean, no offense, but when Jimmy told me he knew someone that could help, I didn't expect a woman."

She'd been waiting for that. She looked at Jimmy. "Maybe this is a good time for me to head out, before I hear any more of this."

"Hold on," Jimmy said. "Leonard, don't embarrass me. I brought you both here in good faith."

She'd been hoping for an out, a way to cut this short without offending Jimmy. A cold meeting like this, with someone she didn't know, was an unnecessary risk. Jimmy would know that. She wondered if age and illness had taken their toll, warped his judgment.

Leonard rubbed a knee, squinted out the window, making a decision.

"No offense," she said, "but I don't have a lot of time."

He looked back at her. "I'm not sure how much Jimmy told you."

"Nothing," she said.

"What it is, I might have a line on some money that was stashed away years ago. A lot of money."

"Might?"

"That's just it. I've been away awhile. Things may have changed."

She was liking it even less now. "Away?"

"Not what you think. Just out of state. But I'm from back here originally, Queens. Problem is, I don't really know anyone around here anymore. Except Jimmy. Nobody I can trust, at least. So forgive me if I'm a little paranoid."

"Where were you?" she said.

"Not the joint, if that's what you're worried about."

She let that pass. He was playing it close, not giving more than he had to.

"Tell me about the money," she said. Wanting him to move it along, bring them to a place she could say no.

"It's been out of circulation awhile. As far as I know, no one's found it. If they had, I would have heard."

"Whose money?"

"It's from a robbery. A long time ago."

"How long?"

"Thirty-five years."

Jimmy held up a hand. "Hold on," he said to her. "It's not as crazy as it sounds. I can back up part of the story, at least. I was around back then."

Leonard shifted in his seat. "If she doesn't believe me, maybe it's better we don't get into it at all."

"Fine with me." She stood. "Sorry, Jimmy."

"Stop," he said. "No need for all this. Leonard, say your piece. If neither of you likes what you hear, you can both walk away, no hard feelings."

Leonard leaned forward, steepled his hands, looked at her. There was something familiar about him. Not someone she'd met, but someone she'd seen, in a photo maybe, or on television.

"All right," she said. She sat back down.

"That's better," Jimmy said. "Now, Leonard, let's hear it."

Leonard tapped his fingertips together, looked at the floor, then up at her. "You know about Lufthansa?"

"The airline?"

"The robbery. Back in '78. Biggest cash heist in U.S. history at the time."

"I've heard of it."

"Six guys walked into the Lufthansa cargo terminal at JFK, walked out with eight, maybe ten million in cash and jewels. That was the estimate, at least. None of it was traceable."

"Where'd the money come from?"

"People changing currency overseas. Military, tourists, whatever. The jewelry was being couriered, for delivery to the States. Just a coincidence it was there that day. The score was mainly cash, though. Most of it was never recovered."

"And won't be at this point," she said.

"Leonard's got a theory on that," Jimmy said.

"Let's hear it," she said.

"Some of the money got spread out right away," Leonard said. "Up here and in Florida. Tribute to the bosses, and then some into a kind of investment fund. Seed money for businesses, real estate, that sort of thing. But there was still a lot left over. So people got greedy."

"You know all this how?" she said.

"I was part of the crew that did it."

She sat back. This was different. "You one of the six?"

"No."

"But you got your share."

He shook his head. "Should have, but didn't. Things got crazy right afterward. Guys started getting whacked right and left."

"I remember that," Jimmy said. "It was a bad time."

To Leonard, she said, "Go on."

"The guy who put it together, Jimmy Burke—we called him 'the Gent'—he kicked up to Joe Diamante, Joey Dio. Joey oversaw a bunch of the Queens crews back then, along with Tony Ducks and Paulie Vario."

She recognized the names. "You knew all these people?"

"I was around them. I used to be at Roberts Lounge all the time, in Ozone Park. That's where we all hung out, Jimmy and the guys. We sat around, shot the shit. Ran bets out of the back. That's where the whole job came together."

It was all sounding vaguely familiar now. A movie she'd seen, maybe, or a book she'd read.

"Most of those guys from back then are dead," he said. "A couple are in the joint, couple more in the program. Joey Dio just died a few weeks back."

"This is all interesting," she said, "but it's ancient history."

"Joey Dio got a big chunk of the money, maybe the lion's share. It was his territory, so he had to give his blessing in the first place, before Jimmy put the score together. Joey got sent away a few years back, a RICO beef, but word was he'd stashed his cut somewhere, didn't touch it. He was a very paranoid individual. A couple days after the job, he and Jimmy were already having people whacked. It was easier than paying them off."

"They let you walk away?"

He shifted, uncomfortable. "I knew what was coming. So I made some moves first."

"You rolled."

"If you want to call it that."

"What else would you call it?"

"Saving my life. It was me or them."

She looked at Jimmy. He shrugged. "It happens."

To Leonard, she said, "You were in the program?"

"For a while, yeah."

"Testifying in cases? Marshals looking after you?"

"Not anymore. I'm done with all that. No more marshals. Nobody in the G knows I'm back here. And at this point, they wouldn't care. They cut me loose."

"Why?"

"I got tired of playing their game. And they were done with me anyway. I'd been out of the life so long, I wasn't any use to them anymore. The people I knew, the things I did . . . Like you said, ancient history. I'm no good to anybody now."

She could see the regret in his eyes, something close to resignation. As if admitting something to himself for the first time.

"You have family?" she said.

He shook his head. "My wife passed. I don't know where my kids are. I haven't heard from them in a long time."

"You on your own out here?"

"No. I've got someone with me."

"A woman?"

"Yeah."

"And that's it?"

"Just the two of us."

"And your name's not really Leonard, is it?"

"That's the one on my driver's license. And now you know a lot more about me than I do about you."

"What do you know about me?"

"Just that Jimmy vouches for you, says you're a serious person."

She looked at Jimmy again. "I'm still not sure what I'm doing here."

"Since Joey Dio died," Leonard said, "people have been looking for his money."

"Which may or may not exist."

"It exists. I'm ninety-nine point nine percent sure of that."

"And?"

"I think I have an idea where it might be."

"Where?"

He looked at her, didn't answer.

"For what it's worth," Jimmy said, "I knew Joey D a little. That's the way he was. If he had money put away, he'd burn it before letting anyone else near it."

"How much are we talking about?"

"After all this time, I can't be sure," Leonard said. "But I'd guess two, three million at least. Cash."

The numbers made sense. If he'd named a larger amount—six or eight million—she would have dismissed it as unrealistic, made her excuses and left, and apologized to Jimmy later.

"What about his family?" she said. "Someone must have known he had that money."

"His wife died some years back. No kids. He was alone when he passed."

"What about his crews?"

"Most of them are long gone. But there's other guys circling around, getting the scent."

"What's that mean?"

"You need to tell her," Jimmy said.

"Tell me what?"

Leonard shifted again. "Some guys came out to see me, a few days ago. Tracked me down. They wanted me to help them look for the money."

"What happened?"

"They braced me. I got away."

"Where was this?"

"Indiana. Where I was living."

"They still looking for you?"

"Probably."

"They from back east?"

"Brooklyn."

That wasn't good. She looked at Jimmy, then back at Leonard. "So, they could be around here now, waiting for you to turn up."

"Yeah."

"They know you had connections in Jersey?"

"They might."

She turned to Jimmy. "Have you heard anything about all this?"

"Not yet. But I've got my ears open."

He looked younger somehow now, his eyes brighter. She knew what it was. He was in the middle of it again, mediating. Back in the life, broken hip and all.

To Leonard, she said, "You know where this money is? Yes or no?"

"I got a pretty good idea. But getting it, that's something else. I'd need help."

"Where is it?"

He didn't answer.

"What are we talking about?" she said. "A bank? A safe?"

"No bank. A safe, maybe. In a house. My thought was, if I can track it down for sure, we go in together and get it, split it sixty-forty."

"With the sixty to you?"

"Yeah."

"No."

He looked at Jimmy, then back at her. "What did you have in mind?"

"First of all, I haven't heard anything convincing me this money actually exists. Or if it does, that you know where it is."

"You'll have to trust me on that."

"Doesn't work that way. If I'm in it, I'm in it. All the information up front. No surprises later. My decisions, my plans. If we find anything, we split fifty-fifty, expenses off the top, and a finder's fee to Jimmy here. That's if there's anything to find in the first place. Fifty percent of nothing is nothing. You have a cell?"

"No."

"Get a disposable. Give the number to Anthony. I'll get it from him if I need it."

"If?"

"That's all you're going to get from me right now."

She turned to Jimmy. "Is that all right with you?"

"Of course. I appreciate your coming here."

She stood, put a hand on his shoulder, felt the sharp bones there. "Take care, Jimmy. We'll talk soon." He patted her wrist.

Out in the hall, Anthony pushed away from the wall. As the door swung shut, she could hear them talking inside, voices low.

"Walk with me," she said.

He fell in beside her. At the elevator, she said, "You know that guy in there?"

"Never seen him before. My grandfather must trust him, though, or he wouldn't be here."

"I hope you're right."

They rode down in silence. She believed Leonard—or whatever his name was—about the crew he'd run with, his part in the robbery. He looked the type, a New York wiseguy forty hard years down the road. But where the money was now, or even if it existed, was another thing.

Out in the parking lot, Anthony nodded at a brown Volvo sedan. She followed him. The day was cold, the sky cloudless.

When they reached the Volvo, she said, "Not what I would have guessed."

"You expecting a Lincoln?"

"Maybe."

"This is my Dadmobile. I'm a dad."

He unlocked the door, got behind the wheel, leaned over and opened the glove box, came out with a thick legal-size manila envelope.

"It's all in here. But like I said, if I were you, I'd ditch those twenties soon as you can."

She slipped the envelope in her coat pocket. "Thanks."

"Sorry the news wasn't better."

She looked up at the sky. "I should have expected it, way my luck's been running lately."

"Maybe it's getting ready to change."

"Maybe," she said. "But I have my doubts."

# ELEVEN

She opened the envelope, shook out the money on the kitchen counter. He'd marked the bad bills with tiny Xs in the lower left-hand corners. She took a closer look at those bills, noted the paper was slightly brighter, the printing less sharp than on the others.

She divided the money into two piles. The real bills came to $9,880. She exhaled. There was nothing for it. What was gone was gone.

She disconnected the kitchen smoke detector, burned the bad twenties in the sink. She took her time, only adding another bill when the previous one was almost gone. She watched them curl and smoke, Andrew Jackson's face darkening, then disappearing, in the hungry flame.

When she was finished, she opened a window to vent the smoke, turned on the faucet. The ashes swirled, dirty water circling the drain.

She got her laptop, opened it on the kitchen table. Her cell buzzed. Rathka's number.

"What did you find out?" she said.

"A little. But I need to ask you again: Are you sure you're okay?"

"I'm fine. What do you know?"

"Cavanaugh's in custody. Possession with intent. His two associates too, one with a gunshot wound. Newark police are still trying to sort it all out. I think the assumption is, it was a drug deal gone wrong."

"Close enough," she said. "Are they talking?"

"Not that I've heard. Cavanaugh will post bond, though, if he hasn't already. For the others, too. You could be in danger."

"I'll take my chances. This isn't over. But I'll deal with it when I'm ready."

"What's that mean?"

"He owes me money."

"Your best bet right now is to stay as far away from him as possible."

"I will," she said. "For now. But sooner or later, this gets settled. It's not just about the money."

"No," he said. "I guess it never is."

When he ended the call, she powered up the laptop, logged into the house's Wi-Fi signal. She went to a search engine, typed in LUFTHANSA ROBBERY 1978. A list of stories filled the screen. She clicked on the first one and started to read.

When he opened the passenger door and got in, she said, "Should I call you Leonard or Benny?"

He shut the door. "Up to you, I guess. Where are we going?"

"For a ride, talk a little." They were in the parking lot of a Target store just off the Garden State Parkway. She'd gotten there an hour before they were supposed to meet, parked and waited, watching the lot. He'd shown up on time, alone, in a battered green Hyundai with Indiana plates.

She started the engine, pulled out of the spot. The sky was slate gray, rain coming soon.

"First thing you need to do," she said, "is get rid of that car. Or at least the plates. If someone's looking for you, you won't be hard to find, driving around in that thing."

"It's the only car I've got."

"Figure something else out. It's no good."

She circled the lot, eyeing the rearview.

"I wasn't followed, if that's what you're worried about," he said.

"You sure about that?"

"I kept an eye out. Like I said, I'm a little paranoid these days."

"I don't blame you, from what I've read." She got on the Parkway ramp, headed south.

"How much do you know?" he said.

"Enough. I did some research. Then I talked to our mutual friend again."

"And?"

"He backs up your story, as far as it goes."

"Then you definitely know more about me than I do about you."

"Way it'll stay for the time being, I'm afraid."

"What do I call you?"

"Linda's fine."

"That your real name?"

"It's the one on my driver's license."

"Fair enough."

She slowed as they crossed the Driscoll Bridge, wind pushing against the car. There was a service area ahead. She signaled for the exit, watched the rearview. No one followed them onto the ramp.

"Why are you stopping?" he said.

"This is as good a place as any."

She drove past the main building and the gas station, found a spot at the far end of the commuter lot.

She shut the engine off. "Okay, Benny. Let's talk."

"We're just gonna sit here?"

"Clock's ticking."

Wind blew grit against the car. He looked out the window.

"Maybe I'm having second thoughts," he said.

"About what?"

"Jimmy vouched for you and all, but I still don't know much about you. How do I know this isn't all a setup, that you work for the G?"

"I could ask you the same, with better reason. After all, you did work for the G. How do I know you don't still?"

"I can give you my word, for what that's worth. More importantly, Jimmy may be an old guy now, but he still knows a lot of people. If I scammed him on this, even now, he'd find a way to put a hurting on me. It would only take a couple phone calls. Why would I risk that?"

"Good point. So where's that leave us?"

"Trusting each other, I guess. At least for a while. So, you did some research. You know I wasn't bullshitting you."

"I know what happened. It's the aftermath I'm unclear on. And where you fit in."

"Okay." He shifted to face her. "There's been a lot written about those days. Some of it's true. A lot of it's bullshit. The crew I was with back then, we were out of Queens, near the airport. We were boosting swag from there all the time, grabbing the trucks as soon as they left the cargo area. We bled that place dry."

"Didn't figure you for a stickup guy."

"Most of them were give-ups, where the driver was in on it. It was a good gig. Nobody really got hurt, if they were smart. I was a kid then, twenty-two, twenty-three, making a couple grand a week. Big money back in those days."

"Big money now."

"Never could hold on to it, though. Always my problem. Booze, broads, clothes, cars. Coke, for a while."

"Jump ahead."

"Sorry. Good times for the most part. I was living it up, thought it would never end. Guys like me, we ruled the city back then."

He looked out at the cars passing by on the Parkway.

"I worked my way up. I was a good earner. Gambling, taking bets, then finally fixing games. That's where the real money was. A lot easier on the nerves, too. Then, a bookie I know came to me, said he had this guy who was into him for a lot of dough. He couldn't pay, so instead he told him about this score he had all set up, was just looking for someone to do it."

"The airport."

"Yeah. This guy worked there, knew the operation. He had the whole thing mapped out. It sounded good, too. I passed it on to Jimmy the Gent. He wasn't exactly a skipper—he couldn't be, because he wasn't Italian—but he was the equivalent, you know?"

"You worked for him?"

"I was under his wing, put it that way. He liked me, because I had an eye for the angles, could figure things out. But the Gent, he was no slouch, either. A very intelligent guy. Generous with his friends, too, as long as you didn't get on his bad side. Not somebody you wanted mad at you."

It was all more than she needed to know, but she let him tell it, not wanting to interrupt him now.

"Jimmy liked the airport score. He started putting a crew together, working out the details. First he had to get approval from Joey D, who ran things around there. Even so, the whole job came together in like a month."

"What was your part?"

"I brought it to him, that was it. I wasn't in on the planning. When it finally happened I wasn't even in New York. I was up in Maine on a bullshit gambling charge when it all went down."

"In custody?"

"Nah, out on bond, waiting for trial. Jimmy had promised me a finder's fee. A good one, too. I was thinking about buying my own McDonald's on Queens Boulevard. No shit, really. You could buy in for, like, fifty grand then. It would have been a gold mine."

"What happened at the airport?"

"Jimmy picked seven guys. Six to go in, one to drive the van."

"Too many."

"Maybe. Way it turned out, you're probably right. Three A.M. when they went in, so there weren't many employees around. They tied up the ones that were there, made the supervisor open the vault. Cartons of money in there, mostly fifties and hundreds. They grabbed everything they could, loaded the van, got the hell out of there. It was sweet."

"Sorry you missed out?"

"Nah. By that point, waving a gun around wasn't my idea of how to make a buck. When I heard about it, though, I couldn't believe it. They thought they were going to take two, three million out of there. Turned out to be more like ten, nobody really knew for sure."

A car crossed in front of them, looking for a parking spot. They watched it go by. When it was gone, she said, "You get your finder's fee?"

"No. Things started to fall apart right away. People were disappearing, getting whacked. Somebody would bug Jimmy for their share, and then a couple days later they'd vanish. I was smart, I kept my mouth shut. Except for Jimmy, just about everybody who touched that money got dead."

"What happened to it?"

"Like I said, some of it got split up among the various bosses, passed around. Joey Dio got the biggest cut. There used to be a rule of thumb: For every million you steal, you sit on it one year. To be safe. But Joey took that to the extreme. He sat on it all for, like, thirty years."

"You're sure of that?"

"It's the way he was. If he'd started spending that money, word would have gotten around, especially with the feds watching him all the time. He lived in the same house, on Staten Island, for forty years. Never spent anything that anybody could see. Some bosses, they would invest in a business, or put money out on the street. Joey never did any of that. He was too greedy."

"None of that's proof the money's still around."

"There's a second part to the story." He took his glasses off, wiped them with a tissue, adjusted them, worked them back over his ears. She waited.

"Couple years ago, when I was still in the program, this FBI agent came out to see me. Young guy, too young to have been around back then, but all he wanted to talk about was Lufthansa. Said he was working with the DEA on a big case back east, and some bills had turned up they thought might be from the airport haul. Hundreds and fifties, old style, dates going back to the sixties, seventies. Money that should have been pulled from circulation long ago."

"Where did they find it?"

"I couldn't get a lot out of him, except it was a meth thing, biker gangs down in South Jersey, Philly. There was a big bust, and they seized a lot of cash and product. Some of those bills were mixed in with the money. But they didn't get anywhere with it, so the whole thing ended there."

"You're losing me," she said.

"This FBI guy thought, since I was on the G's pad, I was everybody's punch. He wanted me to come back east, help him connect the dots. That was the last thing I wanted to do. I had a life where I was, a good job. I was off the booze and the dope, working the steps. Getting my shit together for the first time in my life."

"What did you tell him?"

"The truth. That I didn't know jack about biker gangs, or meth, or any of that stuff."

"What did you know?"

He chewed his lip, didn't answer.

"What's wrong?" she said.

"I'm putting myself in a jackpot here, aren't I? I mean, if I tell you everything, then what do you need me for, right?"

She was buying the story so far, wanted to hear more. But she needed to handle him carefully. He was skittish now, but she couldn't give him the upper hand, let him think he was calling the shots on what to tell her, what to leave out.

"What I'm thinking is, maybe this was all a mistake," she said. She started the engine. "I'll take you back to your car."

"Wait a minute. Can you blame me? I mean, you're not even in yet, right?"

She looked at him, waiting him out.

"Okay, just hold on," he said. "Shut the engine off."

She did. "You've got about thirty seconds to say something that makes sense."

"You know, if it wasn't for Jimmy Peaches, I wouldn't even be talking to . . ."

"Twenty-five."

"Take it easy. Yeah, I have an idea where that money is. But others will figure it out soon, too. Maybe they already have. We'd have to move fast."

"Tell it."

"Joey D was divorced. His wife caught him banging this woman was, like, eighteen years younger than him. He'd been on and off with this broad for years. Everybody knew about it. It was a big scandal, because the wife was the sister of a Gambino guy. Joey lost a lot of respect for that, almost got whacked himself."

"So?"

"While he was waiting for the verdict to come in on his RICO case, he went on the lam. They finally nabbed him way up in North Jersey, a motel near the New York border, out in the woods, middle of nowhere. My guess is, that's where he went when he knew they were closing in. To lead them away."

"From what?"

"From where he'd really been hiding out."

"And you know where that was?" She heard far-off thunder.

"Back in '78," he said, "right before Lufthansa, the Gent tells me Joey needs a favor, something out in Jersey. Wouldn't say what. I drive all the way out there with Frankie Utrecht, another guy from our crew. Takes like three hours to get up there. Joey meets us at a bar in the middle of the sticks. Pickup trucks out front, gravel parking lot, you know? We stick out like nobody's business. Turns out he's having some issues with a construction company there, independent. They got no idea who Joey is, and they're stalling on a project he's got going. They're building a house, but it's taking too long, and the price keeps going up. Joey wants us to go, get them motivated, but not use his name."

"Why?"

"He had his reasons. So we go talk to these people. Family-run business, you know? Been in the same place for fifty years. New York, that's like another world to them. But they're not trying to screw Joey, they're just having problems getting all the materials he wants. So Frankie and I go out there, talk to them, and it gets settled. A month later, the house is finished, everybody's happy."

"I thought you were done strong-arming by then."

"I was. I went in there with a suitcase full of cash. Fifty grand went pretty far in those days. It let them know we were serious, and it also soothed their feathers. That was the easy way to do it."

"Whose money was it?"

"It came from our crew. Joey never knew about it. I talked to the Gent, and he said, 'Fuck it, go up there and straighten it out, tell me how much cash you need.' It was a favor to Joey. Joey says he needs something, you do it. You don't need to tell him how. He doesn't want to know how the sausage gets made."

"What about the house?"

"He had the girlfriend stashed there. House was in her name. It was a place he could go be with her, or stay if he needed to lam it. Jimmy told us to keep our mouths shut, not tell anyone what we'd done, where we'd gone. And I never did. Until right now."

"What about your pal Frankie?"

"He went in on the airport thing. He was one of the first to get whacked. I started to panic because I could see what was happening. Now Joey and Jimmy had two reasons for wanting me dead. My finder's fee—which they weren't going to pay—and the house in Jersey, because now I was the only one who knew about it, besides them. I never got past high school, but you don't need to be a genius to figure that one out."

"What was the girlfriend's name?"

"Brenda Scalise. At least that's what she was using back then."

"She could be long gone."

"Maybe. But the motel where Joey was arrested was only about two miles from that house. And that was less than five years ago."

Rain began to spot the windshield.

"You know the address?" she said.

"Not the exact number. But it can't be hard to find. I know the town."

"Did you meet her? Would you recognize her?"

"Saw her once or twice. Once she was giving the builders some shit about the back deck, getting stain on the grass or something. As far as recognizing her, I don't know. Maybe. That was a long time ago."

"A lot of maybes," she said.

"All fits together, though, don't it?"

"One thing I don't understand."

"What?"

"You."

"What's that mean?"

"You gave up the life years ago, right? Went straight, lived off the government."

"You think it was that simple?"

"Now you want to be a player again, risk your life going after some wiseguy money others are already looking for. Doesn't make sense."

He looked out the window again, low thunder rolling around them.

"I've got nothing anymore," he said. "I had a life out there, a job, friends. Now I don't. They took all that away from me, and there's no way I can get it back. I need to start over. I can't do that broke."

She thought about Wayne, walking out a prison gate in a few weeks, if they were lucky. They would need their own stake to start again, new names, a place to live. It would cost a lot more than the few thousand she had left.

"How do you see your part in this?" she said. "You're not twenty-three anymore."

"I'll do whatever I need to do."

"This woman you're with."

"Marta."

"How much does she know?"

"Some of it."

"She expecting a cut?"

"It's not that way. She's with me."

"Then she's your responsibility."

"I understand that."

She started the engine. "I'll take you back now."

"If you want," he said, "we can go up there this week, take a look around, see if the setup's the way I remember it, if the woman's there. Then you can make your decision."

They got back on the Parkway, drove without speaking. The rain began to pick up, sounded on the roof. She was putting it all together in her head, the whole thing crazy enough to be true.

When she pulled into the Target lot, he said, "Well?"

She rolled to a stop near his car. "I'll think on it. We might have another conversation. We might not."

"You're starting to like the sound of it, though, aren't you? Maybe just a little."

She didn't answer.

"That's okay," he said. "That's good enough for now."

He got out, shut the door, pulled his coat tighter around him. She watched him walk to his car in the rain.

# TWELVE

Benny was feeling good when he opened the motel room door. He started to call out to Marta, then saw the man with the gun sitting on the bed.

"That's all right," Danny Taliferro said from his left. "Come on in."

The door closed behind him. He thought of his Colt, in the trunk of the Hyundai, hidden in the wheel well. No use to him now.

Taliferro was in the desk chair, wearing a white turtleneck and a dark overcoat. The man on the bed was a stranger, with buzz-cut hair and the flat nose of a boxer. He had a long-barreled revolver in his lap.

Benny felt cold. "Where is she?"

Marta's voice came from beyond the half-open bathroom door. "Benny?"

He started for it. The door opened wider, and Frankie Longo was standing there, a bandage over his left eyebrow, scratches on the bridge of his nose. A blue-steel automatic hung from his right hand. Behind him, Marta sat on the edge of the bathtub, her hands bound in back.

The man with the revolver said, "Hold on there, slick," and got off the bed. He came up behind Benny, patted him down.

"I'm sorry," Marta said.

"It's okay, baby. Are you all right?"

"She's fine," Taliferro said. "For now."

The one with the revolver said, "He's clean."

"This is Perry," Taliferro said. "Dominic couldn't make it. He's still not walking so good, thanks to you."

He got up, rolled his right shoulder, massaged it. "Still a little stiff myself. I was lucky. Couple arteries in there you could have hit. And it was a week before I got all the hearing back in that ear."

"What do you want?" Benny said.

"What do you think?" Taliferro said. "Have a seat, talk to us."

Longo came closer. Benny's mouth was dry. "I still don't know anything," he said. "I can't help you."

"Maybe, maybe not," Taliferro said. "But it's not just about that anymore, is it?"

To Longo, he said, "Go easy. And give me that thing. I don't want you losing your shit."

Longo handed over the gun. Benny took a step back, his legs heavy.

"Don't break his jaw," Taliferro said. "We need him to talk."

Longo came toward him, and Benny tried to back up again. Perry blocked his way.

"Wait a minute," Benny said. "Let's just—"

Longo's open hand flashed toward him. He heard Marta cry out, and suddenly he was on the floor, his face stinging, his glasses gone.

"I said easy," Taliferro said.

"That *was* easy," Longo said. Then to Benny, "Get up."

Benny didn't move. The copper taste of blood was in his mouth. Stay down, he thought. Cover up, take what's coming.

"You're fine," Longo said. "That was nothing. Get up."

Benny stayed where he was.

"Do what he says," Perry said. "Get up." He brushed Benny's ear with the muzzle of the revolver. When Benny didn't move, he cocked the hammer, the sound loud and close. Benny could smell gun oil.

He rolled onto his knees, the room tilting around him. He got one foot under him, then the other, and stood.

"That's right. Come on," Longo said. "You're the tough guy. The OG."

"Leave him alone," Marta said.

"Keep that broad quiet," Taliferro said. Perry went into the bathroom.

"Don't hurt her," Benny said. "She's got noth—"

Longo's hand flashed out again, and Benny found himself falling. The wall stopped him. He tried to get his elbows up to protect his face, and Longo crowded in, slapping with both hands until Benny was dizzy and reeling.

He started to fall, and Longo put fingers on his chest, pinned him against the wall. Benny tried to raise his arms, numb from the blows they'd caught. He drew in breath, heard a wheeze deep in his chest, felt the first surge of panic.

"Right there," Longo said. The hand came back up, but it was a fist this time, something white wrapped around the knuckles. Benny tried to turn away, and then the air blurred in front of him. The room spun fast on its axis, and threw him off into darkness.

\* \* \*

Crissa was parked in the motel lot, watching the door of Room 18. She'd followed Benny here, seen him go inside, the curtains already closed. He'd parked the Hyundai right out front. Careless.

The radio was tuned to QXR, a Bach cello piece coming softly from the speakers. She'd wait awhile, see if he came out, if anyone came out with him.

The rain was steady now, streaming down the windshield. She thought about what he'd told her. If it was all true, it might be easy work, a couple million lying there, waiting for someone to take it. If they didn't move on it, someone else would. If she waited too long, weighed all the angles, it might be snatched out from under them. But Benny was the key. She couldn't do it without him.

The curtains parted, and a man she didn't know looked out, scanned the lot, then drew them closed again.

She sat up straight. That's it, she thought. Whoever that was, whatever's going on in there, the deal's blown. Drive away. Call Jimmy, tell him it's off.

She started the engine, looked at the room door. Law inside, maybe. Or more likely the men that had tracked him down in Indiana, followed him all the way back here.

She let out her breath, thinking it through. If they were still after him, then the story was probably true, the money real. But if she left now, she'd never know.

She took out her cell, dialed 411, got the number of the motel. When the desk clerk answered, she asked for Room 18. The line began to buzz.

On the sixth ring, someone picked up. Silence, then a faint noise in the background, a woman crying out. The hard smack of flesh on flesh, then silence again. A male voice she didn't recognize said, "Yeah?"

"Sorry, wrong room." She hung up. So Benny's woman was in there, too.

She pulled out of the parking space, circled the lot. Nothing that looked like a surveillance vehicle, no service vans with generic company names. In the back lot, parked out of sight behind a Dumpster, was a glistening Lincoln Town Car with New York plates, no one inside.

She drove around again, backed into the same spot, shut off the engine. She took the Tomcat from her coat pocket, eased back the slide to check the shell in the chamber. She thumbed off the safety, put the gun back in her pocket.

Take off, she thought. Staying around here, not knowing the situation, was too much exposure. Go back to Avon, get your things, head out. Phone Jimmy from somewhere safe.

She felt irritated, angry. Something else being taken away from her. First the mess in South Carolina, then Cavanaugh, now this. A long string of bad luck. Events pushing her along as if she had no control over them, no choice, her fate already decided. All of it getting away from her before she could fix it. Everything going to hell.


When Benny woke, Perry was hanging up the phone. "Wrong number."

Benny's face was numb, his bottom lip swollen. His tongue found the split there, tasted blood. He felt dizzy, nauseous.

From behind him, out of sight, Taliferro said, "Anyone else know you're here?" When he didn't respond, Taliferro put a foot on his hip, rocked him. "Wake up. Answer me."

"No," Benny said. His voice was strange, hoarse. He twisted on the carpet, felt the warmth then, looked down to see the stain across the front of his pants. He'd wet himself.

"Where have you been all day?" Taliferro said. "We been waiting here a long time. We were getting restless."

Longo squatted in front of him. He was chewing gum. There was a white hand towel knotted around his right fist. "Listen up, rat. The man's talking to you."

Benny opened and closed his eyes, Longo swimming in and out of focus. He saw his glasses under the dresser a few feet away. Then he remembered Marta, twisted to look toward the bathroom. The door was closed, Perry standing outside.

"She's all right," Taliferro said. "I had to give her a little slap to shut her up, that's all. Perry wanted to take a run at her. Hell, I might have, too. Long time since I had a piece of trim that young. But I said no, business first."

"I'll bring her out here, do her right on the bed in front of him," Longo said. "That'll get him talking, I bet. She'd probably like it, too. A good stiff one for a change."

"See what I have to put up with?" Taliferro said to Benny. "These young guys, that's all they think about. Thing is, the longer you make us wait around, the more they'll need some distraction. Then I can't guarantee anything, you know what I mean?"

Benny put his hands on the floor, sat up, fighting the urge to be sick. There was a solid knot of pressure in the center of his chest.

"So, who'd you go to see today?" Taliferro said. "Who you been talking to?"

Benny had to swallow before he could speak. "Nobody."

Longo took Benny's chin in his hand. "Hey, shitbird. Are you aware of what's going on here? We got all night."

"Ease off," Taliferro said. He dragged the chair around in front of Benny, sat. Longo stood, backed away.

"You're lying to me," Taliferro said. "And I always know when I'm being lied to. It's like a sixth sense, you know? I think you've been going around, talking to people from the old days, seeing what you can find out. Am I right?"

Benny swallowed again. "I told you the truth, Danny. I don't know anything about that money."

"Out in Bumfuck, I maybe half bought that line. But here, forget about it. You know where it is, or you know how to find out, or you wouldn't be here. You'd be in fucking Mexico, looking over your shoulder, waiting for me to ride up on your ass."

"Danny, believe me . . ."

"That's just it," Taliferro said. "I don't. Part of me wants to pop you right now for everything you did, get it over with. But I don't have that luxury, you know? I need you. And that pisses me off."

He nodded at the bathroom. "But her, that's another story. Her I don't care about. These boys can pull a train on her until the sun comes up. It would serve her right, tagging along with a rat fuck like you."

"I haven't talked to anyone," Benny said. "I swear on my mother." He coughed, and a blood bubble came to his lips. He couldn't seem to get enough air in his lungs.

"All right," Taliferro said. "If that's the way you want it." To Perry, he said, "Get the girl out here. Gag her first."

"Forget about the gag. I've got something else that'll do the trick."

"Whatever. Just keep her quiet."

There was a knock at the door.

Everyone froze. The knock came again.

"What the fuck?" Longo said.

Taliferro looked at Benny. "You expecting anyone?"

"No." Hoping whoever it was would keep knocking, not go away. Give him the chance he needed.

Longo crossed to the window, parted the curtains slightly. "Some broad. Probably got the wrong room."

"That was a woman on the phone, too," Perry said. "Maybe it's the same one."

The knock came again, insistent.

"Ignore it," Taliferro said. "She'll go away."

Another knock, then the knob rattled.

"She ain't going away," Longo said.

"Get him in the bathroom with the girl," Taliferro said. "Shut them both up."

A louder knock, a fist this time.

Perry grabbed Benny's arm, hoisted him up, the gun in his other hand. "Get in there."

Benny drew in breath, ready to shout. Perry stuck the muzzle of the revolver into his ribs. "Don't be stupid."

With the next knock, the door shook.

"Bitch don't give up," Longo said. He unwrapped the towel from his hand, dropped it in the wastebasket.

Perry opened the bathroom door, pushed Benny inside. His knee gave out, and he went down onto the tile. Marta came off the tub, knelt beside him. "Benny, are you hurt?"

"Just lay there, and shut the fuck up," Perry said. He showed them the revolver.

The pain was solidifying in Benny's chest. He sucked in air. You're having a heart attack, he thought. After all you've been through, you're going to die right here, like this. Right in front of her.

Perry pulled the door shut, stood over them. He put a finger over his lips, cocked the revolver.

* * *

Crissa smiled at the man who opened the door, said, "You Steve?"

He had a bandage above one eye, scratches. He looked her over, his glance drifting down to her wet sweater.

He shook his head, popped gum. "Got the wrong room."

"I'm supposed to meet Steve," she said. "He told me Room Eighteen. This is Eighteen, right?" She looked over his shoulder at a silver-haired man standing near the closed bathroom door, hands in his overcoat pockets. Near his feet, under the dresser, was a pair of glasses.

"Yeah, but there's no Steve here," the man with the bandage said. He started to close the door, and she took out the .32, touched the muzzle to the center of his forehead and said, "Back the fuck up."

He looked at her, at the gun. She thumb-cocked the hammer.

"Careful with that," he said. He took a step back, and she followed him into the room, let the door shut behind her.

"Hold on there," the older one said. There was an edge of hoarseness in his voice. "Who are you?"

She stepped to the side to cover them both. To the older one, she said, "Take your hands from your pockets. Slow."

"I got a pistol in here," he said. "I'm taking it out. Don't get nervous."

"Put it on the dresser, then back away."

He drew a dark automatic from his pocket. "Here you go." He set it on the dresser, stepped back.

"We're cops," the one with the bandage said. "And if you don't put that thing away, you're going to be in a lot of trouble."

"Shut up." She moved around him, picked up the automatic. It was a Browning .380, wouldn't need to be cocked. She pointed the .32 at the bathroom door.

"Tell whoever's in there to come out slow," she said. "I can shoot both of you in the time it takes to open that door."

"I believe you," the older one said. "Perry, come on out. Not too fast."

"Lady, listen to me," the one with the bandage said. "You're in deep shit."

"Let's everybody take it easy now," the older one said. "Everybody stay calm. Perry, come on. It's okay."

The bathroom door opened, and a man came out, one hand out of sight behind him. She pointed the .32 at his chest. "Whatever you've got there, put it on the bed. Slow."

He looked at the older one, who nodded. "Do what she says. We're all gonna talk."

The man lifted a revolver, set it on the bed, backed away.

"Benny," she said. "Come out here."

She heard him moving around inside. Her vision seemed to constrict, her world shrinking to the three men in front of her, the guns in her hands.

Benny came out slowly. The left side of his face was swollen, his bottom lip split.

"Under the dresser," she said. "Don't get in front of me."

He stayed clear of the others, bent and picked up his glasses, put them on. He went back into the bathroom, limping slightly, and came out a moment later, leading a woman whose hands were tied behind her back. She was younger than Crissa expected, wearing jeans and T-shirt, her blond hair loose. There was a fading red mark on her left cheek.

"Get your things together," Crissa said. "Do it fast."

"Wait a minute," the older one said. "Now that we're all calmed down, let's talk about this."

The one with the bandage was watching her. This wouldn't last, she knew. One of them would make a move soon.

"Benny," she said. "Come here."

"Yeah," the one with the bandage said. "Do what she says, Benny. Before you get smacked again."

She put the .32 in her pocket, switched the Browning to her right hand. With her left, she took out her pocket knife, a short-bladed Buck, handed it to Benny. "Cut her loose."

"Do you know who that is?" the older one said. "What's he's done? You really think you can trust him?"

"Car keys," she said.

"What?"

"Car keys. Put them on the dresser."

"I don't have them."

"Who does?"

"Frankie," he said. "Give her the keys."

The one with the bandage said, "They're in my coat. On the bed. I'll get 'em."

"Stay where you are," she said.

Benny was cutting through the plastic flex-cuffs that bound the woman's wrists. When he was done, she pulled away from him, massaging her wrists. They were red and welted. He closed the knife.

Crissa got the revolver from the bed, her hands full again, said, "Benny, get the keys."

The girl moved fast. Benny reached for her, but it was too late. She struck Frankie full across the face with an open hand, nails scraping his cheek. He grabbed her wrist, pulled his other hand back to hit her.

"Don't," Crissa said. She pointed the Browning at his face. "Let her go."

The girl pulled her arm back, and when Frankie let go she stumbled away, almost falling. Benny caught her.

"Bitch," Frankie said. He touched his face, fingertips coming away with blood. There were two red lines along his cheek, just below his left eye.

It was time to go. Crissa backed away, keeping the bed in front of her. It would slow them down when they made their move.

"What's your name?" the older one said.

To Benny, she said, "Get your things. Now."

He got two suitcases from the closet, opened them on the bed, pulled clothes from dresser drawers. The girl stood by the door, rubbing her wrists.

"My name is Danny Taliferro," the older one said. "Maybe you heard of me."

"No," Crissa said.

"Ask around, and you will."

Benny closed the suitcases. He went through Frankie's overcoat pockets, came out with a set of Lincoln keys on a leather fob.

"You know who you're partnering with there?" Taliferro said. "Who he is?"

"We're ready," Benny said. He and the girl were at the door, suitcases in hand.

"Outside," Crissa said. "My car."

"Let me tell you about this guy," Taliferro said. "He's got a long history of fucking over his friends."

"He's a piece of shit, is what he is," Frankie said. He'd moved closer.

"Go on," Crissa said to Benny. "Go."

They went out into the rain. The door shut behind them.

"Listen to me," Taliferro said. "That guy ratted out his partners to save himself. He'll rat you out, too, after he gets what he wants."

She backed toward the door. Frankie had taken another step toward her.

"You got some balls coming in here like that," Taliferro said. "I respect that. You know my name now. You come find me. Maybe we got some common ground. We can talk this out."

"I don't think so."

"But we will, sooner or later. There's nowhere you can go we can't track you down. We found him twice now. You think we can't do it again?"

She stuck the revolver in her belt, reached back with her left hand, felt the doorknob.

"If you don't come see me," Taliferro said, "then I'm going to have to go find you. And that won't be so nice."

She opened the door. "Anyone comes out after me gets a bullet in the head."

"I'm not going anywhere," Taliferro said. "I'm just going to sit right here." He straightened the chair, sat. The others were watching him, as if waiting for a signal.

She went out fast, pulled the door shut. Benny and the girl were waiting by the Taurus.

"Get in," Crissa said. "Hurry." She got out her keypad, unlocked the doors.

There was a storm drain by the car, water swirling down below. She popped the magazine out of the Browning, slid the gun into the drain, heard it splash. The revolver and the magazine went in after it.

Benny and the girl were already in the backseat, crowded in with their suitcases. Crissa got behind the wheel, started the engine, peeled out, tires kicking up water. She watched the motel in the rearview, waiting for someone to come after them.

The girl's face was white. "Who are you?"

Crissa didn't answer. She got on the highway, headed west, wipers thumping. When the motel was out of sight, she said, "Give me those keys."

He handed them up to her. She powered the window down, tossed them out. Thunder sounded above them.

The girl touched Benny's face gingerly. He winced.

"Either of you need a doctor?" Crissa said.

"No," he said. "I think we're all right."

"Good."

She merged onto the Staten Island Expressway, cut quickly across two lanes of traffic, still watching the rearview. There was always the chance they had another set of keys, another car. She moved into the passing lane, gunned it, the Goethals Bridge in sight ahead.

"My car," Benny said.

"Forget it. And whatever name you used to check into that motel, forget that, too. It's no good anymore. What else did you leave behind?"

"An overnight bag. But there wasn't much in it. I think we got everything important."

The girl clung to his left arm, holding it tight. There were tears in her eyes, all of it hitting her now. She put her head on his shoulder, began to shake. He kissed her hair.

Crissa changed lanes again, signaling for the exit that would take them onto the bridge and into Jersey.

"I don't know how they found me," he said.

"Keeping the car was foolish," Crissa said. "It would have been easy to track. Using it was a mistake."

"They were there about the money."

"I guessed."

"So now you know I was telling the truth."

"Jury's still out on that," she said.

In New Jersey, they got on the turnpike, headed south. A few minutes later, there were signs for the parkway entrance. The rain was heavier now, the traffic slowing. Night coming quick.

"You followed me all the way back there?" he said. "I never even saw you."

"I'm not surprised. I wanted to see where you would go. Who you were with."

"But you came in. You didn't have to. You could have just driven away."

"I thought about it."

The girl was sniffling. Crissa opened the glove box, took out a small plastic package of tissues, handed it back. The girl took it, blew her nose loudly, wadded up another tissue and wiped her eyes. Benny rubbed her back gently.

"This is Marta," he said. Crissa nodded at her in the rearview.

"Whoever you are," Marta said, "thank you. For coming in. For not driving away. You saved our lives."

"This time," Crissa said.

"It was all my fault," he said. "Getting myself into that position. Making it easy for them. I'm forgetting things I used to know."

"Then start remembering," Crissa said. "You're going to need them."

# THIRTEEN

They were in Crissa's kitchen, Benny with a New Jersey map spread out on the table. He looked it over a moment, then pointed to a spot in the top west corner. The side of his face was darkening into a bruise.

"Your memory that good?" Crissa said.

"That's the place. Sussex County. Like I said, middle of nowhere."

Marta was on the living room couch, arms crossed tight, Benny's coat around her. Rain blew against the windows.

Three hours since they'd left the motel. She'd driven back to Avon by a circuitous route, making sure they weren't followed. Marta was calmer now. She'd made coffee for all of them, happy to have something to do. But Crissa could see the exhaustion in her eyes.

Benny drank from his mug. Crissa nodded at Marta. "You sure she's all right?"

"I think so," he said. "Angry more than anything."

"At you?"

"Maybe."

She sipped coffee, looked at the map. The place he'd pointed out was equidistant from the New York and Pennsylvania state lines, the Delaware River a border to the west. It would be a two- to three-hour drive from Avon. She read town names: Colesville, Plumbsock, Libertyville. Patches of green between them with no names at all.

"Rural area," she said. "Tough to operate there without calling attention to ourselves. We'll have to stake the house out, watch it, maybe for a week or more. And we have to find it in the first place."

"I can find it. I'm sure of that."

She traced a finger along the routes out of town. Local roads to Route 15 South, then another twenty miles before they reached Interstate 80, and the straight run east.

"We can't wait too long," he said. "Danny and his crew will be looking, too. He may already know about the Scalise woman, where she is."

She shook her head. "I don't like this. Too many things we don't know."

"Worth going up there to take a look, though, isn't it?"

"Tell me more about this Taliferro."

He sat back. "I've told you most of it. He used to be a capo, worked for a guy named Patsy Spinnell."

"Used to be?"

"Patsy's been gone a while. Most of his people are in jail, or dead. Danny's on his own now, runs some sort of renegade crew, doesn't answer to anyone. He's got a rep, though, goes way back."

"What's that mean?"

"You see the scar on his throat?"

"No."

He ran a finger above his Adam's apple. "Piano wire. Late seventies. He got into a beef with a crew out of Flatbush. One night they caught him alone in a bar in Maspeth, two of them, like three in the morning. They came up behind, put a wire around his neck. He wasn't carrying, he never did back then. Fought them off with his bare hands, killed both of them, got cut up pretty bad in the process. But it sent a message."

"What was that?"

"That he didn't die easy. That if you came looking for Danny Taliferro, you better bring an army."

"What kind of a crew does he have now?"

"I don't know. Even back in the day, it was like eight, ten guys at most. They were heavy hitters, though, and loyal. Danny used to work out of a bar he owned in Canarsie, place called the Victory Lounge. That was his headquarters. Don't know if it's still there. That was a long time ago. A lot of bad shit happened in that place."

"Like what?"

"It started as a typical wiseguy joint, left over from the fifties. If you went in for a drink, they'd charge you like ten dollars for a beer, just so you got the message, 'Don't come back.' Lots of deals went down there, scores got planned. But there was an apartment on the second floor, above the bar, that Danny used for other things. Guys went in there, never came out."

"Go on."

"Danny was Patsy's chief hitter. You got on Patsy's bad side, you had to worry about Danny and his crew coming after you. He wasn't afraid to do the heavy work."

He looked over at Marta, lowered his voice. "Word was people got hacked up in there, in the apartment. Danny and some of the others would do it right there, in the bathtub. Six pieces—arms, legs, chest, head. They'd put the parts in suitcases, leave 'em in the Fountain Avenue dump. Or maybe weigh 'em down, take a boat out, drop 'em in Sheepshead Bay."

"Nice friends you had."

"No friends of mine. It was crazy back then, before the feds started putting away all the bosses. Some outrageous shit happened. Guys like Joey Dio, Patsy—they ran the city. Nobody could touch them. And if you were affiliated with them, forget about it. They were the kings, and the rest of us, we were like the princes. Anything we wanted, we got."

"Until you end up in a suitcase."

"Why do you think I went over to the G? After Lufthansa, when people started disappearing, I knew it was only a matter of time."

Marta came into the kitchen.

"How you doing, baby?" he said.

She took the chair next to him, hooked her arm through his. She touched his face. "We should put some ice on that."

"It's okay. Just a little sore."

Crissa looked at Marta's wrists, the welts there starting to fade. "You sure you don't need a doctor?"

"I'm fine. But I still don't know who you are."

Crissa looked at Benny. He took one of Marta's hands, said, "She's a friend."

"How do you know Benny?"

"I didn't, until a couple days ago," Crissa said. "We have a mutual acquaintance."

"Are we safe here?"

"For now. Better than being out on the street. You two can take the bedroom tonight, I'll sleep on the couch."

"I don't want to put you out," he said.

"Don't worry about it. How'd they get in?"

"It was my fault," Marta said. "The one who knocked at the door, Perry, I'd never seen him before. I would have recognized the others. He told me he was with the police. Then the other two pushed their way in."

He squeezed her hand.

"You were lucky," Crissa said. "Things could have gone bad in there."

Marta brushed hair from her eyes. "I'd say they got pretty bad as it was."

"You're angry," Crissa said. "That's good. Hold on to it."

Benny slipped an arm over Marta's shoulders, squeezed.

Crissa folded up the map. "I have to go see someone tomorrow. I want you two to stay here. Don't go out for any reason. Not even to walk around, look at the water. There's food in the refrigerator. When I get back, we'll talk more."

"We shouldn't even be here," Marta said. She looked at Benny. "We should go someplace far away, before they find us again."

"We will, baby. But it's like I told you—"

Crissa got up. "I'll leave you to it. Let me just get some things out of the bedroom."

"Give us a gun," Marta said.

Crissa looked at her. "What?"

"When you go tomorrow, to see whoever you have to see, leave us a gun."

"I don't think so." Crissa looked at Benny, then back at her. "A gun can get you into more trouble than it gets you out of."

"You've got one," she said.

"That's right."

"We should have one, too."

"You don't need one."

"Are you so sure of that? After tonight?"

Crissa didn't answer. There was nothing to say to that.

The clouds were gone, the morning bright. Crissa pushed Jimmy's wheelchair along the boardwalk. The ocean was flat and calm, sunlight flashing off the surface. Gulls circled overhead.

"Let's stop here," he said. "Take a rest."

She parked the chair beside a bench, locked the wheels. She'd told him what Benny had said, about the Scalise woman, the house. How Taliferro had tracked him down again.

He took a Portofino tube from his coat pocket, unscrewed the cap. "Thanks again for these."

He slid the cigar out, got a silver lighter from another pocket, opened it, thumbed the wheel. Wind blew out the flame.

"Let me," she said. She took the lighter, cupped it with her other hand, got it going.

He lit the cigar, puffed. "Thank you." She closed the lighter, slid it back in his pocket, sat on the bench. He drew on the cigar.

"It's good to get out like this," he said. "I get tired of being around all those old people. It's depressing."

A jogger was coming along from their right, sneakered feet thumping against the boards. He wore a headband, earbuds, an iPod strapped to his upper arm. He nodded at them as he went by.

When he was gone, Jimmy said, "So what are you thinking?"

"I'm not sure. I guess it's worth looking into. But there are other factors."

He tapped ash from the cigar. "That Taliferro. He's a son of a bitch, excuse my language. Always was. The worst of the worst."

"You know him?"

"Met him once or twice. He had a reputation, even way back then. I never understood guys like him though. I mean, this is supposed to be a business. Where's the percentage in whacking some poor slob, cutting up his body? All that does is bring heat. If somebody has to go, he has to go. But you do it right. You do it clean. And that's only if there's no other way around it."

"I braced him. He knows me now, by sight at least."

"That's too bad. But Benny's right, Taliferro's on his own. Not connected the way he used to be. He's got some half-assed crew around him, but that's about it. He might not have much in the way of resources."

"Good. Because the last thing I need right now is to get into the middle of some wiseguy shit I need a scorecard to figure out. I had enough of that last time."

"I understand."

"And I'm not sure how much I trust our mutual friend."

"Benny and I go back a long way, that's all I can tell you. Made some money together. He was a good earner. Those people he was with, though, they didn't respect that. They were animals."

"That justify what he did? He was a rat. He testified against his friends, went into witness protection."

Jimmy pulled on his cigar, took it from his mouth, rolled it in his fingers. "He did."

"I'm surprised you'd even talk to him now."

"Who knows?" he said. "If the circumstances were different, it might have been me."

"I can't believe that."

"The man had a target on him."

"That's what he said."

"He was right."

"How do you know that?"

"Because I had the contract." He let smoke out, looked out over the water.

"What happened?" she said.

He raised a hand dismissively, let it fall.

"Joey D and the other one, the Gent, they knew Benny and I were friends. They thought I could get him to come down to Jersey. Let him get comfortable, think he was safe, then have one of my guys take him out. That's the way they do it. They always use someone you trust."

"They tell you why?"

"Just that he was talking to the G, could hurt a lot of people. But I knew it was about the airport thing."

"What did you do?"

"Nothing. I stalled. I knew he was gonna turn. Was hoping he would, at least. There was no other way out for him. If he'd tried to run, they'd have found him."

"You tipped him off?"

"More or less." He blew smoke out. "I'd seen it coming, too. Whenever a crew starts whacking people without good reason, you know they're on their way down. Only a matter of time before either the feds are all over them, or they start taking each other out for some bullshit or other, usually about money. Once you start killing, it's hard to stop."

"So he owes you."

"Maybe. I believe him, though, about Joey's money. It's what I'd always heard, too. That he'd salted it away, didn't touch it."

"A lot of ifs," she said.

"If he's right, though, it would be a sweet score. Even a piece of it, if that's all that's left. All cash, can't be traced. How often is that the case these days?"

"Not very."

"Have a look, listen to your instincts. You'll know whether it's right or not. You're a pro."

"These days, I'm not so sure about that."

"I am." He touched her arm, then took his hand away.

"You need to be careful yourself," she said. "If this Taliferro starts putting things together, he might guess Benny's been down here. Especially since you were friends back in the day."

"I've already spoken with Anthony about that. We'll deal with it as it happens. Is there anything you need?"

"Maybe. Depends on what I decide."

"Whatever you want, let Anthony know. He can help you out with that."

He puffed on the cigar. After a moment, she said, "You had this all planned."

"I'm sure I don't know what you mean."

She smiled. "You're still a sly one, aren't you?"

"Just keeping my eyes open."

"That makes two of us," she said.

# FOURTEEN

There was a recreation area at the bottom of the hill, tennis courts, outbuildings. Crissa parked in the lot there, and together they started up the trail, Benny panting after the first few minutes.

They'd driven the area for the last hour, and she'd picked this hill as the best vantage point for a view of the house. After talking with Jimmy yesterday, she'd decided there was nothing to be gained by waiting. They'd left Marta in Avon, gotten an early start that morning. By noon, they'd found the driveway that led to the house, Benny's memory as good as he'd claimed.

"You okay?" she said.

"I think so. Just let me rest for a minute."

They came out into an area with picnic tables, rusty grills. The sun was high, but the wind had teeth. She wore her leather jacket, gloves. Around her neck was a pair of binoculars she'd bought at an army surplus store in Asbury Park.

He sat on a wide rock, hands on his hips, catching his breath.

"You have any health issues you need to tell me about?" she said.

He shook his head, but didn't look at her. "Nothing besides old age."

"You're doing pretty good for sixty-two."

"It doesn't feel like it."

The park was open until dusk, but they'd seen no one else on their way up. Other than the wind, the only noise came from traffic on the county road down below.

He rooted in a jacket pocket, came out with a prescription bottle, unsnapped the lid. He shook a white pill into his hand, swallowed it, winced. He put the bottle away, looked at the path ahead, which got narrower as it led up through the bare trees.

"What was that?" she said.

"For my allergies. I'm not used to being outside like this."

"Let me see the bottle."

"Why? I told you, I'm fine. Just give me a minute."

"Just so you know," she said, "if you collapse up here, you're on your own. I'm not waiting around for rangers and paramedics."

"Thanks. I'll remember that."

"Tell me again about the woman." Wanting to keep him talking, keep his mind off the way he felt.

"I told you everything I know."

"Maybe you forgot something. What was the situation between them?"

He drew in breath. "She was his *goomara*, his girlfriend. Joey's wife, Teresa, knew about it, but there wasn't much she could do. Brenda was a lot younger than Joey, so I guess that makes her like fifty now."

"Not so unusual, though, was it? A boss having something on the side?"

"No, everybody did. That was expected. But it never lasted. They traded off all the time, handed off their girlfriends to other guys down the ladder. But with this Brenda, it went on for a long time. It was serious. Teresa looked the other way for years, but when they finally got divorced, she really went after him. Got the house in Staten Island, almost everything he owned. He was pissed, but there was nothing he could do about it."

"That doesn't sound like a guy who had a couple million stashed away."

"I'm sure he wanted to keep that money hidden from Teresa as much as from the IRS or the FBI. And like I said, Joey was cheap. It's that Depression mentality. He had it, but wouldn't spend it."

"You ready to keep going?"

"Yeah." He started to get up, sat back. She put a hand out. He took it, pulled himself up. "Thanks."

"If you're having chest pains, something like that, you should go back down."

"No, I'm fine." He dusted off his pants. "Let's go."

They started up the trail again. She could hear his labored breathing as it grew steeper, worrying now she'd made a mistake by bringing him along.

"How's the jaw?" she said.

"It's fine. Couple loose teeth, that's all. I've taken worse beatings for less."

"All part of the life?"

"I'm not complaining. I did what I did back then."

"Was it worth it?"

"For a while, yeah. It seemed that way."

"Doesn't sound it to me. Especially considering how things ended up."

"We all make our choices, right? My father worked in a textile mill in Astoria, on the line, nine, ten hours a day, every day. He went deaf from those machines. I made more money in five years than he did in his entire life. All the work he did, all those hours, everything he sacrificed, he was never anything but poor."

She thought of Seven Tears, the Texas town where she'd grown up. The day she'd left for good had been the happiest of her life. Fifteen years since, and she'd never been back.

"That's the game they want you to play," he said. "Stay poor, work to make someone else rich, then die. When I first started running with a crew, it was like the answer to all that, you know? We threw money around like it was going out of style. When we ran out, we just went and stole some more, pulled some scam, whatever. Not so different from what you do, is it?"

"You have no idea what I do."

"You're right. Sorry. But you know what I'm saying."

"I do."

"You learn it early or you learn it late," he said. "The game's fixed. Nobody gives you anything. You gotta take it."

The path leveled off into a clearing, more picnic tables to one side.

"This is good enough," she said.

At the far end of the clearing, the ground fell away sharply. Waist-high pylons had been driven into the earth there, strung with chains. Three feet beyond was the cliff, gray stone sloping down to the wooded valley below. On the next hill, partly hidden by trees, was the house.

"That it?" she said.

"Looks like it."

She moved into a shaded area, raised the binoculars, focused.

It was a ranch house, but sprawling, as if sections had been added as an afterthought.

The shingles were faded gray, and latticework was missing from the back deck. Tar paper showed through on the roof. There was an attached garage on the far side of the house, a Boston Whaler parked on a trailer beside it. The boat looked new, but it was uncovered, and full of rainwater.

"You see anybody over there?" he said.

She shook her head. The backyard was bordered with dense woods on three sides. A small backhoe was parked there, treads clotted with dirt, construction supplies piled behind it. The stumps of freshly cut trees showed white.

"They're putting in a pool," she said. She scanned the front yard. It was bare dirt, no grass. The gravel driveway ran down the hill, snaked through the trees until it reached the county road below.

Just the three entrances she could see—front door, back deck, and garage. No outside cellar door. No doghouses, water dishes. That was good.

She unslung the binoculars. "Have a look. Take your glasses off. Use the dial to focus."

He put his glasses in a shirt pocket, raised the binoculars, adjusted the dial, then raised them again.

"That's definitely the place," he said. "It wasn't finished the last time I saw it, but that's it. All the money Joey put into it, you'd think someone would have taken better care of it."

"They're doing work there. And that boat's new. Someone's spending money."

"The garage door's going up."

"Let me see."

She took the binoculars back, refocused. A white Cadillac

Escalade with smoked windows and a stainless-steel pushbar came out of the garage, started down the driveway. The door closed slowly behind it.

"New car, too," she said.

"Can you see the driver?"

"No." The Escalade wound its way down through the trees, disappeared from sight. She tracked back over the house, looking for signs of movement in the windows. Nothing. She lowered the glasses.

"What do you think?" he said.

"I need to get online, take a look at the tax records. See whose name that place is in. Could be the woman sold it years ago, and we're looking at some tax attorney's house."

"Odd, isn't it? New boat, new car, putting in a pool, but the house needs a coat of paint? Basic repairs?"

"It is," she said.

"You know what that tells me?"

"Yeah," she said. "Somebody just came into some money."

They stopped to eat on the way back, a diner off Route 80. They were at a booth by the window, the tables around them empty.

After the waitress took their order, he said, "This part of Jersey always makes me nervous. All these mountains. I don't like it."

She watched a tractor-trailer roll past on the highway.

"Way I see it," she said, "here are the problems. First, your information is out of date. We need to find out who's living there, how many people, all that. We have to watch the house, see who goes in and out, and when. That could take a few days."

"All right."

"Second, we need to be able to get in close without being seen. That's going to be tough, because there's only one way in and out of there. Third, we have to get into the house when no one's there, for as long as we need. Fourth, we don't have any idea how long we need. If there is money there, it might be buried somewhere, for all we know, or stuffed down an old well. We could spend days looking for it, never find it."

"It's in a safe, I'd think," he said. "In the house."

"Why?"

"That was one of the issues with the builders. Joey wanted an extra room off the basement, with a reinforced concrete floor. He didn't say why, and it didn't mean anything to me at the time. Now it makes sense. My guess is, after the builders were done, he had someone come in, install a safe."

"Why am I just hearing this now?"

He shrugged. "Didn't occur to me."

"Anything else you're holding back? If so, now's the time. Any more surprises down the road, and we're going to have an issue."

"No more surprises. You know everything that I do."

"If there's a safe, we'll need a boxman."

"You know any?"

She thought of Rorey, lying dead on a concrete floor in South Carolina. "Not anymore."

"You know the best way to get into a safe?"

"What's that?" she said.

"You put a gun to the owner's head and say, 'Open the fucking safe.'"

"That the way you used to do it?"

"Me? Nah. I was never that kind of thief. I never had the balls. You, on the other hand . . ."

The waitress came back, refilled their coffee. When she was

gone, Crissa said, "We'll need a base around here. Someplace we can stay without being noticed, for as long as it takes. Not too close, but not far away, either. We may need to split up, so we'll have to get you a car, too. I'll put it on my card, we'll take it out of expenses if we ever see any money. You're no use to me if you're not mobile."

"What about Marta?"

"She can stay down at the house. Safest place for her right now."

"I don't like leaving her alone."

"It's no good having her up here with us. Just another complication. We've got enough as it is. She'll be okay. Just make sure she stays put."

"So we're really gonna move on this."

"You want out, say it."

"Maybe Marta's right. That the smart thing to do is get away from here, from all this."

"You can still do that."

"You'd go through with it anyway, though, wouldn't you? If I left? You don't really need me anymore."

"I'm not sure what I'd do. If you're thinking about backing out, and you want a finder's fee—on the chance I take anything out of there—then maybe we can work that out. But I can't do this alone. If you're out, I need to bring in someone else, maybe two people. That means the split is less. But there's no sense talking about money until we know for sure there's some there."

"I did kind of put this whole thing in motion, though, didn't I?"

"You did. And you'd get something for that. But putting something in motion isn't the same as pulling it off. You don't need me to tell you that."

"No, I guess I don't. It's kind of ironic, isn't it?"

"What?"

"It's like full circle. All those years ago, how this whole thing got started. Someone came to me with a plan, something that was ripe. All that money there, waiting to be grabbed. And I came to you the same way."

"There's one difference," she said.

"What's that?"

"I probably won't kill you afterward."

"That's comforting."

The waitress brought their food, and they ate in silence. Crissa was running it all through in her head, the approaches to the house, how to get up there, what she'd need.

"You have kids?" he said.

She looked at him. "What's that got to do with anything?"

"Just curious. I've got two, a boy and a girl."

"You told me."

He pushed his plate aside, hamburger half eaten, and looked out the window. He wanted to talk now, so she'd let him. She needed him to think of her as a partner, that they were bound together. Not off on his own, having second thoughts about it all. If talking helped, she'd do it.

"I have a daughter," she said. "She turned ten last month."

"She live with you?"

She shook her head.

"With her father?"

"No. She's with family. A cousin."

"You miss her?"

"All the time." She finished her steak. The waitress refilled their cups, took the plates away.

"Kids," he said. "You owe them, you know? For bringing them into the world. You have a responsibility to them, to make sure they're safe, that they've got a fair shot. I don't think I did a very good job with that part."

She wondered where this was going, how much to give him in return.

"You do what you have to," she said. "You make the decisions you think are right, based on the information you have at the time. There's no percentage in looking back."

"Yeah, but I guess I look at things differently now. With Marta especially. Like maybe for the first time in my life, I'm thinking about someone other than myself, what I need, what I want."

"Good for you."

"Yeah, took long enough, didn't it? It was like a wake-up call one day. I saw who I was, what I'd done, what I'd lost. Knew I had to make some changes. I did the twelve steps, the whole deal."

"How'd that work out for you?"

"Got me on the right path. Got me started. Didn't stick with it, though. Couldn't handle those meetings, bad coffee and stale donuts, listening to those people go on and on. It worked for a while, but I needed to get away from it. Couple stumbles along the way, but I've been sober pretty much ever since. Six years now."

"Congratulations."

"Marta's helped. She had my number from the start. Don't know what I'd do without her, where I'd be. Thing is, being honest with other people, treating them right, none of that comes naturally. Looking out for yourself comes easy. Everything else, you have to work at."

"I guess that's true."

It was almost dark. They drank coffee, watched the traffic on the interstate. She was restless. Things to do tomorrow, to get ready. No more time to waste.

"What now?" he said.

"Back to Avon. I have a couple errands to run tomorrow, places to go. I want to be back up here the day after, find a motel, get organized."

"I know I'm the one started all this. But being up here now, seeing the house and all . . . I'm getting a bad feeling about it."

"It happens," she said. "Sometimes it's real. A warning. Something your subconscious is picking up that you aren't. Other times it's just fear, static."

"How do you know the difference?"

"That's the thing," she said. "You don't."

The hardware store was in Newark, on Broad Street, three blocks down from the gold-leafed dome of City Hall. She went up a narrow flight of stairs, and through a glass door with a cardboard OPEN sign.

There was a middle-aged black man behind the counter, his hair solid gray. He wore bifocals on a cord, was reading a newspaper laid out in front of him. There was no one else in the store.

He looked up as she came in. "Help you?"

"Maybe. Are you Otis?"

He slipped his glasses off, let them hang.

"My friend Anthony called," she said. "Told you I'd be coming by."

He looked past her at the door. "Is that right?"

"He said to tell you his father says you were the best center Weequahic High ever had."

He frowned. "Jimmy Junior said that?"

"That was the message."

"When was the last time you saw him?"

"I've never met him. He's in Marion now. I know his father, Jimmy Peaches. Anthony's grandfather."

"You're not what I expected."

"Sorry. Can you help me out or not?"

"Why don't you flip that sign, lock that door?"

She turned the sign to CLOSED, worked the two deadbolts.

"So you know Anthony," he said. "And you know who Jimmy Junior is. But how do I know who you are?"

"You don't." She took a cash-stuffed envelope from her coat pocket, set it on the counter. "Those are my credentials."

"You come on strong, don't you?"

"No more than I have to."

"Come on back here. We'll see what we can do."

He opened the counter flap for her, gestured at the doorway that led into a back room.

"You first," she said.

"All right." He limped ahead of her. She took the envelope from the counter, followed him.

The room beyond smelled of sawdust and solder. Metal shelves rose toward the ceiling. Propped in one corner was a mannequin wearing a full-length bulletproof vest.

"Weequahic," he said. "That was a long time ago."

She looked around the room. There was a sawed-off double-barreled shotgun on pegs just above the door. She wondered if anyone had ever tried to rob him, what had happened when they did.

"Our friend didn't give me much of an idea what you need," he said.

She pointed at the vest. "How much you asking for that?"

"Five hundred. Price might be negotiable. You interested?"

"Just curious. You get much call for that? People coming in off the street, looking for body armor?"

"All the time. Just what is it you want?"

"Looking for a handheld," she said. "Something with a little push. Nine-millimeter or better."

She'd keep the .32 as a backup, but couldn't count on its stopping power. She thought of the snub-nosed .38 Wayne had given her, now rusting at the bottom of a Connecticut river.

"Wheel gun or auto?" he said.

"Either. Let's see what you got."

He took down a box marked PIPE JOINTS from a shelf above his head, set it on a workbench. He opened the flaps, reached into foam peanuts, drew out a rag-wrapped bundle, and set it on the table. He did it twice more, the cloths spotted with oil.

Inside the first bundle was a Colt .357 revolver with a ventilated barrel. The other weapons were automatics, a Glock .40, and something she didn't recognize.

"What's that?" she said.

"GSh, Russian."

"Looks cheap."

"It ain't."

"This all you have?"

"For now. Couple weeks, maybe something else."

The Colt was too big for practical purposes. She picked up the Glock, worked the slide. It was smooth, well oiled. She ejected the empty magazine, thumbed the loading spring to check the tension. The gun looked new, felt right in her hand.

"You looking for something bigger?" he said.

"What do you mean?"

He limped to a shelf across the room, came back with a long box, unmarked. He set it on the table, took the lid off, pushed rags aside. Inside was a short-barreled Remington 12-gauge pump, black and chrome.

"Model 870," he said. "Almost new. Might let it go for the right price. I was holding it for someone, but I don't think he's coming back."

She shook her head. "Maybe some other time."

"Suit yourself."

"How much for the Glock?"

"That all you want?"

"For now."

"Eight hundred."

"Six."

"Then I guess it's a deal. Seven."

"Shells?"

"How many you need?'

"Two boxes. Three if you've got them. And a spare magazine."

"I can do that."

She paid him with hundreds from the envelope. He wrapped the gun in the rag again, put it along with the extra magazine and three boxes of shells in a cheap canvas gym bag, zipped it shut.

"You tell Anthony I was sorry to hear about his father. I did my share in state lockup, when I was younger. But federal, Marion, that's hard time."

"I'll tell him."

She let herself out, walked down Broad to where she'd parked the Taurus. Late afternoon and the sidewalk was crowded with office workers on their way home, people leaving the nearby courthouse. A line was queuing at the corner bus stop. By six o'clock, this would be a ghost town, the street empty, most of the buildings dark.

She stowed the bag in the trunk, shut the lid. She waited for cops to come out of alleyways and unmarked vans, guns drawn. People moved past her on the sidewalk, none making eye contact. You're paranoid, she thought, the way you always get before you commit to something. But maybe this time that's a good thing.

Driving south on the Parkway, she called Rathka. When Monique put him on the line, Crissa said, "What do you hear?"

"On which front?"

"All of them."

"Two of our friends are out on bond. You need to be careful."

"You, too."

"I am. There's a fellow works for me from time to time, an ex-Jersey state trooper. I've got him out there watching the Montclair house. It's not cheap, but it makes me feel a whole lot better."

"I'm sorry," she said. "I feel like I brought all this on."

"Occupational hazard. Sorry I had to turn you away in the first place. I've been having second thoughts about that."

"Doesn't matter now. We need to think about our arrangement going forward, though."

"You expecting something soon?"

"Maybe. Looking it over."

"If it happens, we'll figure something out, come up with a plan."

"That's good to hear. What about Texas?"

"I heard from our guard down there. He's concerned our friend is going to force an issue with the fellow he's been having problems with. He says word on the tier is it's heading that way."

"Can't they do something? Put him in Ad Seg until his hearing comes up?"

"If he asked, they would, I'm sure. But until he does, I don't imagine they're going to do much of anything."

"I don't want him getting hurt," she said. "Not now, of all times."

"Nobody does. Our guard's looking out for him, when he's on shift, but there's not much else we can do."

"Can you set up another call?"

"I can try. When were you thinking?"

"As soon as possible. I may be out of town for a couple days."

"Business?"

"Maybe. I'll let you know."

"Well, don't let me know too much. . . ."

"Don't worry," she said. "I won't."

# FIFTEEN

At noon the next day, she was parked at a small strip mall on a wooded stretch of county road. Even without the binoculars, she had a clear view of the driveway a quarter mile ahead.

On the far side of the lot, Benny was parked beneath a stand of trees, out of sight of the road, in a green Honda Civic she'd rented that morning.

She was in the passenger seat of the Taurus. It was less suspicious this way, would look as if she were waiting for someone. The strip mall held a laundromat, a paint store, and a flower shop, but the first two had few customers, and the shop never opened.

Her cell buzzed. Benny's number.

"Yeah?" she answered.

"How long are we going to wait here?"

"As long as it takes."

"What if no one comes out today?"

"Then we come back tomorrow, do the same thing."

"I'll need to piss soon," he said.

"You still have that thermos full of coffee?"

"Yeah. You want some?"

"No. Dump it out. You can piss in that."

"It'll get all over the place."

"What do you want me to tell you?" she said.

"I bet there's a bathroom in the laundromat."

"No. Stay where you are. I don't want us attracting any more attention than necessary. Use the thermos." She hit END.

She put the phone on the seat, raised the binoculars. No mailbox at the end of the driveway, no address marker. If police or fire/rescue were called, they might just as easily drive by the entrance, especially at night. No mailbox likely meant there was a rented one in town. Someone might eventually head out to check it, allow her to get a look at them.

She'd gone over tax records online the night before. The property was in the name of a B. Scalise, with no sales or changes since the first listing. She'd run the name and address through all the public databases she could access. A Brenda Scalise had applied for a construction permit twice in the last three months, two weeks ago for an in-ground pool installation. So she still owned the property, at least on paper. Who lived there was another question.

Earlier that day, she'd gone to a realty office two towns away, looked at posted listings on the wall. She'd fended off the chatty secretary, reached for a business card on the counter rack, palmed a half dozen of them. The cards were generic: agency name, phone, fax, and Web site.

She set the binoculars down, opened a pocket notebook. On one page, she'd sketched the house the best she could from the vantage point of the opposite hill. Now she used a pencil to fill in the driveway, drew a straight line for the county road.

By two thirty the boredom was getting to her. Few cars had passed. She wondered how Benny had resolved his issue. She was thinking about calling Rathka when she caught a flash of white coming down through the trees.

She speed-dialed Benny. "Heads up."

"What is it?"

The Cadillac came to the end of the driveway, paused there, turned left.

"There goes the Escalade," she said. She read off the plate number. "Stay with it."

"Jesus Christ. Okay, hold on." She heard him fumbling with the phone, then the engine starting. She looked across the lot, saw him pull out. He bumped onto the road, started after the Escalade.

"Not too close," she said. "Just enough to keep it in sight."

"How far should I follow it?"

"As far as it takes you."

"What if we end up in Pennsylvania or somewhere?"

"Then call me from there," she said, and hung up.

She climbed over into the driver's seat, reached down, and pulled out the Glock from where it had been wedged into the springs there. She tucked it into her belt in the back, the tail of the sweater covering it.

Slipping off the gloves, she wiped her damp palms on her jeans legs. She gave it five more minutes, to see if anyone else came out of the driveway. Then she pulled the gloves back on, started the engine.

No traffic on the road. She pulled out, checked the rearview. Nothing coming up behind. She slowed, made the left into the driveway.

It was wide and rutted, and she could see the tracks where

they'd brought up the backhoe. She had to slow almost to a stop to negotiate the curves, the driveway growing steeper.

When the house was in sight, she pulled off into the trees, killed the engine. There would be just enough room to turn around, head back down.

Her phone buzzed. Benny again. "What is it?"

"She just pulled into a bank, went inside," he said. "I got a pretty good look when she got out of the Escalade. I think it's her. What do you want me to do?"

"Go in after her. Fill out a deposit slip, whatever. Keep an eye on her. If she turns around, starts heading back here, you need to call me. Do you think she'd recognize you?"

"After all this time? I'd doubt it."

"Be careful."

"I'm going in now," he said, and ended the call.

She opened the glove box, took out the small digital camera she'd bought the day before. She got out of the Taurus, locked it, started up the driveway.

Woods on both sides, the shadows deepening. When she reached the yard, she activated the camera, took three quick shots of the front of the house. She'd upload them to her laptop later, blow them up for better detail.

No security cameras she could see, no sign of an alarm system. At the garage, she looked through the window, saw an oil-stained concrete floor, a closed door that led into the house.

She took shots of the garage, the boat, then the backyard and deck. A sliding glass door with vertical blinds led into the kitchen. To the left of the deck was a window with a broken and sagging miniblind. Through the gaps, she could see a small den, the living room, and the front door beyond. There would be a half dozen ways to get inside, if she needed to. It would take five minutes at most.

She circled the house, took more shots. On the way back to the car, her phone buzzed.

"She left the bank," Benny said. "I think she's heading back. I'm right behind her."

"It's okay, I'm done." She got behind the wheel, started the engine. "What did she do in there?"

"Brought in a gray canvas money bag, kind with a zipper. Went to talk to one of the bank managers, then they led her into the back. She was in there about fifteen minutes. I was already waiting in the car when she came out. Couldn't stay in there that long, not doing anything."

"Cash deposit," she said. "Safe box."

"Looks like it."

"Meet me back at the motel. We'll talk there."

She ended the call, cut the wheel hard to swing back onto the driveway. As she started down, she heard the throaty cough of an engine ahead. She slowed to take the next bend, and there was a motorcycle there, stopped at an angle across the driveway, blocking her. Black exhaust chugged from its tailpipe.

She braked. The rider wore a leather jacket, jeans, and engineer boots. He undid the strap of a scuffed black helmet, pulled it off, shook out greasy dark hair.

She tapped the horn. He looked at her through the windshield, set the helmet on the gas tank. There was no room to get around him.

He shut off the engine, pushed the kickstand down, climbed off. He wore fingerless gloves, ran a hand through his hair as he came toward her. He was older up close, hair shot through with gray. There was a scar through his left eyebrow.

She powered down her window, eased off the seat so she could reach the Glock if she had to. She kept her left hand on the wheel, right hand on her thigh.

"You're blocking my way," she said.

He didn't answer, looked at the camera, binoculars, and notebook on the passenger seat. He bent to look into the backseat, walked around the car. She thought about hitting the gas, sending the bike into the trees, getting away from there.

He came back to her window. His jaws were working slowly.

"Will you please move your motorcycle?" she said.

He turned his head, spit tobacco onto the dirt. She hung her right thumb on her belt, inches from the Glock.

He looked up toward the house, then back at her. "This is a private road. You're trespassing."

"Is that your house?" she said. "I'm a realtor. I'm new here. I've been looking at some homes in the area, trying to get a feel for the town."

She opened the notebook, took out a card, handed it to him. He looked at it, then spit again. "What's your name?"

"Please move your motorcycle, sir."

On the seat beside her, the phone began to buzz. She ignored it.

"You cold?" he said.

"What?"

"You're wearing gloves."

She didn't answer. The phone went silent.

"Why don't you step on out here?" he said.

"I don't think I want to do that." Her hand touched the butt of the Glock.

He looked at the card again, then slid it in a jeans pocket. "You don't look like a realtor."

"Do I need to call the police?"

"This property isn't for sale. Hasn't been. Won't be. What are you doing up here?"

"I think I already told you that."

"You don't talk much like a realtor, either."

"Is this your property? Are you the owner?"

He looked at her, jaw working, then turned away, went back to the bike. He climbed on, started the engine, spit. He pulled onto the shoulder, out of her way, watched as she drove past.

When she reached the end of the driveway, she turned left onto the county road, wondering if he would follow. A half mile later, she pulled into a dirt turnaround. She was calling Benny when the Escalade passed her, coming from the other direction.

"I've been trying to call you," he said. "She'll be there any minute."

"I saw her. I'm clear."

"You okay?"

"I'm all right." She tugged her right glove off with her teeth, wiped the palm on her jeans. "You get a better look?"

"Yeah. It's her. The years haven't been kind, but I'm pretty sure."

"She see you?"

"I don't think so."

"We've got other complications, too. She's not alone up there. A boyfriend maybe, biker."

He gave that a moment.

"It's the two of them in it together," he said. "Waiting for Joey to die so they could start spending his money. It's gotta be up there somewhere. That's the only way all this makes sense."

"Maybe. But I'm burned. So is the car."

"What do we do now?"

"Part of me says walk away."

"And the other part?"

"We'll talk about that later," she said, and ended the call.

# SIXTEEN

They'd gotten adjoining rooms at a motel forty minutes away. Crissa was at the desk, the laptop open, scrolling through the pictures she'd taken. Benny stood in the connecting doorway, watching her.

"What do we do if there's a safe?" he said.

"We'll have to take our chances with that. Go in strong when someone's home, convince them we're serious. Get them to open it." She looked up. "You ready to do that?"

"It's been a long time since I've gone in heavy anywhere."

"That's why we need to get this straight now. We know there's at least two people in there, maybe more. I can't pull this off myself. I could start looking for someone else to bring in, but that would take time. Time we don't have."

"Why not?"

"Could be she's been putting money away all this time—banks, whatever. There might not be much left. Also, the longer we wait, the more risk we run someone else goes in and grabs it first. Taliferro and his crew. Or maybe somebody we don't even know about yet, who has all the same information we do, and is waiting to make their move."

"Who?"

"I don't know. That's the point. There's too much we don't know. The longer we wait, the less chance we have of bringing anything out of there. at all. So you need to make up your mind. In or out."

When he didn't answer, she said, "And the other option is to cut our losses right now and walk."

"I still think there's money up there. A lot of it."

"That might well be. But the first thing we have to do is get into the house. Then get them to open the safe, with no guarantee there's anything in it. Same amount of work to find out, though. For all we know, she's been depositing money at banks all over the Northeast, and there's nothing left."

"How many banks could she have hit, though, since Joey died? A deposit of ten thousand dollars or more, they have to report it, right? She wouldn't want the IRS after her. At that rate, it might take her a long time to get rid of it. Joey hasn't been gone that long."

"There's lots of places to hide money."

"She's already got a place to hide it. In the house. Why take a chance with it somewhere else, out of her sight? My bet is she'll sit on most of it until she has a reason to move it."

"You saw the Escalade, the boat. She could have been spending the money all along, pissing it away. There's no guarantee what's still up there is worth the effort to take it."

He sat on the bed, rubbed his chest.

"You okay?" she said.

"I'm good."

"What were those pills for, really?"

"Monopril. For my blood pressure."

"You have heart trouble?"

"I had an angioplasty last year."

"If you're not up to this, you need to tell me that now. I can't be worrying about you when things start to jump off. I'm going to have my hands full."

"I understand."

"I'm going to have another look at the place tomorrow, from the trail. You can stay here. I don't need you this time."

"I talked to Marta a little while ago. She's restless, nervous. I can't blame her. She doesn't like being alone."

"Then I guess you have some decisions to make," she said. "And you need to make them soon."

The next day, she was back on the path. She'd taken the Honda, didn't want to risk being seen in the Taurus again.

She sat on a wide flat rock among the trees, away from the path, but with a clear view of the house. She'd brought a bottle of water and three granola bars, had eaten one already. The binoculars hung around her neck.

She heard the motorcycle before she saw it, a distant insect-like buzz, not the full-throated exhaust she'd heard yesterday. She saw movement through the trees, tracked it with the binoculars.

The motorcycle drove into the bare front yard, pulled up near the door. The driver killed the engine, took off his helmet. He was bald and bearded, head shaved clean. She could see an ss tattoo on the side of his neck. He wore a sleeveless denim vest over a black leather jacket.

The door opened, and the rider she'd seen yesterday came out in jeans and T-shirt, barefoot. They greeted each other with soul handshakes and pounds. The dark-haired one had a chromed automatic tucked into his belt in the back. She wondered if he'd had it yesterday, there beneath his jacket.

A woman appeared at the door. She was in her fifties, black hair piled high, smoking a cigarette. She spoke to the bearded man, and then the three of them went inside, the door closing behind them.

Another complication. She sipped water, broke off half of the second granola bar, ate it.

A half hour later, the bearded man came back out, a knapsack over his shoulder. He tucked it into a saddle bag on the rear of the bike, climbed on. The man and woman came out into the yard behind him.

The three of them spoke, then he kickstarted the bike, exhaust and dust billowing up. He wheeled it around, started back down the driveway.

When he was out of sight, the woman turned on the man, making angry gestures, spitting words. He shrugged, went back inside. She flung the cigarette away, followed him.

Crissa lowered the binoculars. Money going out of there, or dope. Or both.

She called Benny. "That South Jersey thing the FBI agent told you about. Where the hundreds came from. Joey ever deal with biker gangs?"

"Not that I know of. Hell, back then we hardly knew what meth was."

"Could have happened since, though, right?"

"I guess. Why?"

"Maybe Joey's girlfriend was running some of that business for him."

"Forget it. Joey was old-school Sicilian. No way he would let a broad handle his money. No offense."

"Maybe she's gone into business on her own since he died. Seed money for meth dealers, or buying and selling it herself."

"Wouldn't surprise me."

"I'm heading back now. You think about what we discussed?"

"Yeah, I have."

"Are you in or out?"

"In, I guess. We've come this far, haven't we?"

"That's right," she said. "We have."

She dressed in near darkness in her motel room. Black turtle-neck, dark windbreaker, sneakers. It was almost midnight, the only light coming from the bathroom.

There was a tap at the connecting door. When she opened it, Benny said, "Are you ready?"

"Almost."

He stared at her for a moment. "You look different."

"How?"

"I don't know. Just different."

She took the Glock from the nightstand, eased back the slide to check the chambered round.

"Why are you bringing that?" he said. "You think you'll need it?"

"No. But I don't want any surprises, either."

"I'm still not sure what we're doing."

"I need to take another look around. I can't go back up there in the daytime." The Glock went into a jacket pocket. "I want a sense of who's in there at night, how many vehicles in the garage. Who's usually awake, and for how late. That's all information we need before we take the chance on going in there. Like I said, no surprises."

She took out a black aluminum penlight, tested it. The beam was narrow but bright. She checked her cell next, switched it to silent mode, put it in a jeans pocket.

"Keep yours on vibrate," she said. "If I need you, I'll call."

"Maybe I should come with you."

"No, stay with the car. You'll be no use to me in the woods. If anyone's awake, they'll hear you coming a mile away. And I want you behind the wheel, ready to haul freight fast if we need to."

She went to the window, parted the curtains. The moon was almost full, backlighting the clouds. That was good.

"Time to go," she said.

# SEVENTEEN

She made her way up through the trees, keeping the driveway to her left. She wore a black watch cap, sweat filming the nape of her neck despite the chill. Benny had dropped her off near the driveway entrance, then gone on to park at the strip mall.

Halfway up the hill, she heard a sharp noise to her right. She stopped, put her hand on the Glock. Holding her breath, she waited for the noise to come again. When it did, she drew the gun, turned to see a deer watching her from a few feet away, eyes glowing in the moonlight. It met her stare for a moment, then sprinted off into the woods. She let out her breath, snugged the Glock back in her pocket.

Ten minutes later, she could see the lighted house through the trees. She pulled back a sleeve to look at her watch. Almost 2:00 A.M. It was then she saw the shape to her left, a darker mass in the shadows. Moonlight glinted off glass.

She moved closer, saw it was a dark SUV with New York plates, parked on the shoulder of the driveway. She took out the Glock, counted off twenty long seconds, then went up on the passenger side. The hood was faintly warm through her glove.

Voices from the house. A shout, then silence.

She took out the penlight, thumbed it on, played the thin beam inside the SUV. On the passenger-side floor was a New Jersey map folded into quarters, a plastic thermos, empty fast-food containers.

She clicked off the penlight, put it away. Voices again, louder now. She moved back into the woods, stepping carefully. Slowly, she made her way to the edge of the yard.

Lights were on in the front windows. The bearded man's motorcycle was parked in the yard.

She moved toward the side of the house, staying in the trees, then crossed quickly to where the boat was parked. Using it as cover, she looked through the garage window. The Escalade was inside, along with the other motorcycle. The interior door that led into the house was open, light coming through. She heard more voices, insistent, then an answer that was something like a sob.

She circled the house. Light came from the den window, spilled onto the ground. A shadow appeared there, from someone inside the house. She pulled back to the wall. The shadow stayed for a long ten count, then moved away.

She ducked beneath the window, came up on the side of the deck, The sliding door was off its track, the vertical blinds tangled. She could see shiny pry marks on the frame.

She moved back to the side yard and the cover of the boat, looked around the corner of the garage. The light through the front windows lit up bare ground.

When the shot came, it made her jump. A shout, then the front door flew open, and the bearded man came out running, hands tied behind him. He wore a white T-shirt, the shoulder sodden with blood.

He'd reached the driveway when a figure appeared in the doorway, lifted a cut-down shotgun. He aimed calmly, fired once, and the bearded man pitched forward onto his face. He moaned and rolled, boot heels scuffing at the dirt.

The man with the shotgun worked the pump, ejected the shell. He stepped out of the doorway, turned his head, spit. He was in his fifties, heavy, wore a green flight jacket.

Another figure behind him now. A familiar hoarse voice said, "You get him, Sal?"

"Yeah," Sal said. The biker was twisting on the ground. "I got him."

"Then finish it."

Sal shifted the shotgun to his left hand, let it hang down. The biker was on his stomach now, trying to crawl into the trees. Sal went toward him, reached under his jacket, drew out a snub-nosed revolver. The biker kept moving, boots pushing against the ground. Sal straddled him, aimed the snub-nose, and fired twice. The biker shook, then lay still.

"Come on," Taliferro said from the doorway. "We're not done here."

Sal spit again, put the gun back under his jacket, went back into the house.

She circled to the den window again, crouched low. She waited, listening, then raised her head and looked through the window.

The woman and the other biker were kneeling on the living room floor, wrists bound behind them. The woman wore a T-shirt and sweatpants, her hair loose and straggly, mascara streaking her face. The man was bare-chested in jeans, thick arms covered with jailhouse tats. Taliferro stood in front of them, Frankie Longo to one side, chewing gum.

Sal waited by the door, the shotgun resting on his shoulder. On the floor were two olive-green duffel bags, big enough to carry golf clubs, zippered shut.

She heard footsteps coming up stairs, and then the man called Perry came into the room, a long pry bar dangling from one gloved hand.

"Nothing else down there," he said. "I checked the walls, floors, air-conditioning ducts, everything. Just the one safe. And it's clean. We got it all."

"Is that right?" Taliferro said to the woman.

"Don't tell him shit," the biker said. He pulled his shoulders back, looked up at Taliferro.

Sal came forward, said, "Smart guy," and drove the butt of the shotgun into the biker's face. The woman cried out.

The biker went over, then righted himself, blood on his lips.

He looked at Sal, spit a tooth on the floor. "Fuck you."

Sal raised the shotgun again.

"Hold off," Taliferro said. Then to the woman, "I was expecting a lot more. What happened, you piss away the rest? Spend all of Joey D's dough on your boyfriend here? Nice Italian girl like you, fucking around with scooter trash?"

"Go fuck your mother, wop," the biker said. "I did." He spit blood on the floor.

Taliferro laughed. "You got some stones, I'll give you that. You must have thought you hit the lottery, huh? Banging Joey's broad, spending his money."

"You got it all wrong," the biker said.

"How's that?"

"It's your sister I was banging. And she loves it up the ass, just like you."

Taliferro's smile disappeared.

"Tough guy," he said. "Maybe you are, at that. But what I don't understand is this meth shit. Selling dope to niggers is one thing. But a white man, selling to white kids. That I don't get."

"Please," the woman said. "Just take the money." She was crying again.

"You ain't gotta worry about that part," Perry said.

"Do what you're here to do," the biker said. "Or get the fuck out."

"Prez," the woman said. "Please. Don't. Just be quiet."

"Sal," Taliferro said, and held out his hand. Sal reached under his jacket, came out with the revolver, handed it over butt first.

"How many did you use?" Taliferro said.

"Just the two."

Taliferro turned to Perry, said, "Get the car. Let's load up."

Perry nodded, went out the front door.

Taliferro looked at the woman. "I'll ask one more time. Where's the rest of it?"

"That's all that's left. I told you what I did with the rest. Why don't you believe me?"

"Tell me again."

"Some I invested. The rest is in banks, safe deposit boxes. I can take you to them tomorrow."

"That's a thought," Taliferro said. He turned back to the biker, pointed the gun at his head. "Prez. That what you called him? Short for Presley, or president?" Prez met his eyes, didn't look away.

"I'll take you around to all the banks," she said. "I'll turn it all over to you. Everything I got."

"How much did you start with?"

"I don't know. However much Joey put in the safe. He never told me."

"He gave you the combination, though. You weren't tempted to go in there while he was alive, take a look yourself?"

"It wasn't like that between us. Joey trusted me."

Crissa wondered if she could break the window, get a clear shot at Taliferro and the one with the shotgun. But the woman was in the way, and Longo was partially hidden from view. All she could hope for was to distract them, take one of them down if she were lucky, buy the woman some time. And then there was Perry out front to worry about. Too many men, too many guns.

"What would Joey think if he saw you right now," Taliferro said. "Trying to protect this piece of shit?"

"You don't know anything about Joey," the woman said.

"I know enough. I know he wouldn't be happy, you spending his money like that."

She squared her shoulders. "If Joey was alive, you'd be pissing yourself right now, knowing he'll come after you for what you did to me."

"Maybe. You're not lying to me now, right? You're positive there's no more here in the house?"

"No," the woman said. "You've got it all."

"This time," Taliferro said, "I believe you."

Crissa turned away, knowing what was coming. Two shots, loud, and then the thump of bodies hitting the floor. Two more shots, evenly spaced.

Silence. Then Longo said, "Jesus Christ, look at all that blood."

"Come on," Taliferro said. "Get those bags. Let's get out of here."

She heard the SUV pull up out front, moved back between the boat and the garage wall, then up to the corner again.

Perry got out of the SUV, opened the back hatch. Longo carried one of the bags out, straining with the weight. He tossed it in, stood aside while Sal came out with the other one. He slid it in beside the first, set the shotgun on top.

"We're all set, skip," Perry said, and shut the hatch. Taliferro came out, and Longo opened the front passenger side door for him. He climbed in, pulled the door shut. Longo and Sal went in the side door. She heard laughter from inside, then the door slid shut. Perry got behind the wheel.

She moved quickly to the back of the house, up onto the deck. With the Glock up, she went into the dark kitchen, toward the light beyond.

The bodies were side by side on the living room floor. She saw the head wounds, knew there was no use in checking pulses or calling 911. Nothing you could have done to prevent it, she told herself. They never had a chance.

She went to the curtains, looked out. The SUV's parking lights were on. It was turning a slow circuit in the yard, headed back to the driveway.

It was over. Whatever money had been in here was theirs now. The whole thing had fallen apart, gotten away from her. Everything gone to hell.

The Escalade keys were on the kitchen table. She grabbed them, went into the garage. She climbed up behind the wheel, started the engine, put the Glock on the seat beside her.

The garage door opener was clipped to the visor. She pushed the button, and the door began to roll up. She hit the gas just as the door cleared head height, felt it scrape along the Escalade's roof.

\* \* \*

Benny had his window open, heard faint noises from the house, knew they were gunshots. So it had all gone bad up there. He waited, listening. Two more shots, and then a final two. Drive away, he thought. She's dead, most likely, and you need to get out of here.

He started the engine, felt pressure in his chest, wished he'd brought his pills with him. He was sweating. He rubbed his palms on his pants, gripped the wheel again, waiting for the pain to ease.

Be smart, he thought. Get out of here while you can. Take the car. Leave her.

Crissa swung the Escalade into the driveway, lights off. The SUV was taking it slow, brake lights glowing every time it reached a bend. She swept the Escalade into the first curve, heard branches scrape the passenger side. She pulled the wheel hard, narrowly missed a tree that loomed up out of nowhere. The seat-belt alert was beeping. She pulled the shoulder harness on, clicked it in place.

Then she was around the last bend, rocks kicking up against the undercarriage, and the SUV was there, at the end of the driveway, ready to turn. She aimed the Escalade at it, floored the gas pedal. The SUV's headlights went on, twin beams springing out into darkness, lighting up trees across the road. It began to turn left.

The Escalade was doing thirty-five when it reached the end of the driveway. She hit the brakes at the last moment, heard them lock and squeal, and the Escalade surged into the road, the steel pushbar clipping the SUV on its left rear corner, exploding glass and plastic, sending it spinning away.

The SUV went into the trees nose-first, and she stayed with it, hands gripping the wheel. She butted the back end hard, drove the SUV deeper into the trees, bulling it forward with the Escalade's weight. The front end of the SUV thudded into a tree trunk, the hood buckling back, windshield spiderwebbing. The airbag bloomed in the front seat.

She backed up, pulled away, switched her high beams on. They lit up the SUV sitting at an angle in the trees, one side higher than the other. One headlight pointed crazily into the woods, the other was dark. Broken plastic and glass littered the ground between the two vehicles.

She got the Glock from the floor, opened the door, climbed down. She pointed the gun at the SUV in a two-handed grip. There was no movement inside.

Closer, she could see Perry and Taliferro slumped in the front seat, the deflated airbag in their laps. The only sounds were the hissing of steam, the tick of cooling metal. She took careful aim, put two shots high through the left rear window, a warning. The glass starred and collapsed.

She went to the hatch—the glass there was gone, the door dented deep from the pushbar. Sal was facedown on the floor by the bench seat; Longo was against the wall, one of the duffel bags across his legs, cubes of safety glass in his hair.

She pulled up on the latch. The hatch opened slowly, the bent metal squealing. Longo was moving in slow motion, pushing the duffel away to free himself. Up front, Taliferro was beginning to stir. None of them had been wearing seat belts.

She pointed the Glock in. Longo looked at her, said, "You." Sal groaned, but didn't move.

With her left hand, she caught the strap of the duffel bag, dragged it out onto the ground, surprised at its weight. Longo cut a glance at Sal's shotgun, which lay against the wall just out of his reach.

She pointed the Glock at his face, picked up the shotgun. New headlights fell across her. She turned, saw the Honda pull up on the shoulder.

She set the shotgun on the ground, pulled out the other bag, dropped it atop the first one, Longo watching her.

Benny was out of the car now. When he saw the wreck, the duffel bags on the ground, he said, "Holy Christ."

"Get these in the trunk," she said.

He stood there for a moment, not moving. She kept the Glock trained on Longo. "Now. Do it quick."

He grabbed one of the duffels, dragged it across the dirt. Sal groaned again.

Maybe this is where you should end it, she thought. A bullet for each of them. The only way to make sure.

Then Benny was beside her, breathing heavy. "I saw head-lights down the road. We need to go."

She backed away, the gun still up. Benny got the second bag in the trunk, shut the lid, leaned on it for a moment, out of breath.

She picked up the shotgun. The barrel had been sawn off even with the pump, the stock cut back to a pistol grip, sanded smooth. She put the Glock in her jacket.

"Come *on*," Benny said. He got back behind the wheel, leaned over, and opened the passenger door.

She racked the shotgun four times in quick succession, emp-tying the magazine. Shells flew from the breach onto the ground, Longo still watching her. Then she reversed the gun, held it by the barrel, swung it hard into a tree, twisting her hips into it. The stock cracked, fell away. She tossed what was left of the gun into the woods.

With a last glance at Longo, she got in the Honda, and said, "Drive."

Benny pulled out onto the road, spraying dirt. "What happened up there?" His face was slick with sweat.

"Nothing good. They're all dead. The woman, the boyfriend, the other one we saw, too. Money's in the duffel bags. What's left of it at least. Slow down. You're going to get us pulled over."

"Jesus."

She still felt calm, focused. Knew it wouldn't last. The adrenaline crash would hit her before long, as soon as they were somewhere safe.

"There's a turnaround up here," she said. "Pull in. I'll drive."

"Where we going?"

"To the motel, get the other car, the rest of our things."

"And then?"

"Home," she said.

# EIGHTEEN

It was almost six when they got back to Avon, dawn a blue glow over the ocean.

Crissa laid the two duffels out on the living room floor. Marta was in the bedroom doorway, hair loose, face still soft from sleep.

"Benny, what are those?" she said. "What happened? Are you all right?"

"I'm fine," he said. "Everything's fine, baby."

Crissa knelt and unzipped one of the bags, saw the money inside. Most of it was banded, but some of the packs had split, spilling out loose bills.

"Now do you believe me?" he said.

She took out a pack, riffled through it. All hundreds. She snapped one out. It was a Series 1977. In the lower right-hand corner, the Secretary of the Treasury's signature read WERNER BLUMENTHAL.

She held out the bill. Benny took it, looked at it. "Oh, yeah."

"Where did all that money come from?" Marta said. "Who does it belong to?"

Crissa unzipped the other bag. It was just as full. Benny whistled softly.

"Come on," Crissa said. She sat on the couch, pulled the first bag closer. "Let's get to work."

It took them an hour to count it. They lined the packs up on the coffee table, used rubber bands on the loose bills. Benny had pulled up a chair. Marta watched from the kitchen.

At the bottom of the second duffel was a black velvet bag with a red drawstring. Inside was a thick necklace laced with diamonds, a matching bracelet.

"Nice stones," he said. "Probably worth a lot."

She set the bag aside. They'd divided the money into two piles, counted each separately. None of the bills was newer than 1977. A third were fifties. There were packs of twenties, but nothing smaller.

When they were done, they compared figures. Both had the same amount: Two million, three hundred and seventy thousand dollars.

"I don't believe it," Benny said.

"We'll count it again."

"How much is there?" Marta said. She'd come out of the kitchen to stand behind him.

"A lot, baby," he said. "A whole lot."

They counted it a second time, came up with the same figure. Crissa did the math. Even split down the middle, expenses off the top, it was the most she'd ever taken down in one shot. It would buy the beginnings of a future for her and Wayne. Maybe one for Maddie, too.

Benny wiped sweat from his forehead. He was pale.

"Are you okay?" Marta said. "You need your medicine?"

He looked at her, not speaking, then shook his head. "No, I don't think so, angel. I think I'm fine." Then he began to laugh.

Crissa looked at the cash, felt a weight lift from her shoulders. For a while at least, there would be no struggle, no financial stresses, no ripping and running.

"What do we do with it?" he said.

She looked up. "What do you mean?"

"Do we just keep it? Like this? Should we transfer it somewhere? Get a bank in the Cayman Islands, what?"

"You're just thinking about that now?"

"To be honest, I never thought we'd get to this point."

"If it's as untraceable as everybody says, you're probably safe," she said. "You can bank some of it, open accounts, as long as you keep the deposits low. You can salt some more away in safe boxes. You'll be surprised how quickly it goes."

He laughed again. "I can't believe this."

"I might be able to put you in touch with someone who'll take it all, put it into investments," she said. "Out of state and overseas. Cents on the dollar, so you'll take a hit. But what you get back will be clean. You won't have to worry about it."

"No. I don't think I'll do that. I think I like it just the way it is."

She stood, knees and hip aching, felt the tension of the last twenty-four hours. Couldn't remember the last time she'd slept.

"Somebody will come looking for that money, won't they?" Marta said.

"Probably," Crissa said. "Which is why you two need to decide where you're going. Don't hang around. If I were you, I'd think Central or South America, Costa Rica maybe."

Marta was staring at the bills. "Is that what all this has been about? The money?"

"That's what everything's about, honey," he said.

"No, it's not," she said. She went into the bedroom, shut the door.

"You can stay here as long as it takes you to get organized," Crissa said. "Then you need to be gone. Safer that way."

"All right."

"We'll do the split now. A thousand off the top for expenses. That goes to me."

"You have receipts?"

She looked at him.

"Just kidding," he said. "A thousand is fine."

"And another fifty grand to Jimmy. His finder's fee."

"Why so much?"

"Because that's how much we're giving him. And that's the way it's going to be."

"If you say so."

"I say so. The rest we split down the middle, as agreed. That's still a million and change for both of us. Be happy with that."

"I am, believe me. What about the jewelry?"

"I have no idea what it's worth," she said. "I'd have to find out."

"You'd have a better chance of moving it than me. Keep it."

For the first time, she noticed the rust-colored spots on one of the bags. They were still wet to the touch. Blood. The woman's or Prez's, or both.

"At the house," she said, "there was a man that Taliferro called Sal. He wasn't at the motel. You know who he is?"

"Older guy? Scary eyes? Kind of blank?"

"That's him."

"Sal Bruno. He and Danny go back a long way. He's a bad guy."

"As opposed to the others?"

"He's worse. He was Danny's cleanup man. They called him 'The Magician,' because he made people disappear. He was the one came up with the suitcase trick. If they brought him along, they weren't planning on leaving anybody alive."

"So how did they find her?"

"Who knows? Maybe someone else knew about her, about the house. Maybe they just put two and two together, same way we did, decided to give it a shot, go talk to her."

"Then why go all the way out to Indiana to brace you?"

"I don't know," he said. "Maybe he didn't know at first. Maybe somebody she knew sold her out. A lot of people would do a lot of crazy things for a piece of that money."

"They already have," she said. "Us, too."

They counted out Jimmy's money first, hundreds bound in five-thousand-dollar packs. She took twenty fifties for the expenses, then divided the rest equally, split it between the duffel bags. It came to one million, one hundred and fifty-nine thousand each.

She'd drawn the blinds over the sliding glass door, but light still filled the room. Benny was taking individual bills from his banded packs, holding them up.

"What are you looking for?' she said.

"Fugazies. Counterfeit. I wouldn't put it past Joey, his last joke on everybody."

"Find any?"

"Not yet."

She went into the kitchen, opened a bottle of Medoc, poured a full glass.

"This bother you?" she said. She touched the bottle.

"No, go ahead, enjoy. Almost wish I was still drinking, today at least. This is something worth celebrating."

She thought of the three people she'd seen die that night. "Not feeling that way myself."

"You should be. This is a once-in-a-lifetime score, the kind people like us dream about, right?"

She took the glass into the living room, nodded at the bedroom door. "She going to be all right?"

"She'll be better when we're away from here. We've got a stake now at least. Something that'll last her even after I'm gone. She deserves it, all I've put her through."

She sat on the couch. "You going to get married?"

"We've talked about it, but I don't know. Sometimes I think she doesn't know what she's gotten into, with the age difference and the health thing. But she'll realize it sooner or later. She's young, she'll want to have kids at some point. And I'm too old for that."

"Maybe not."

"No? I remember when I turned forty. I can tell you exactly what I did that night, where I went, what I drank. Twenty-two years ago, but it feels like yesterday. Twenty-two years from now, though, I'll be eighty-four, if I make it that long. You get to be my age, the math works against you."

"You're no different from anybody else." She drank wine.

"And there's this heart thing, too. It's been okay for a while. I take my meds, watch my blood pressure and all that. But that could change tomorrow. I don't know how much time I have left."

"Who does?" she said.

He put the money back in the duffel, zipped it up. "What about your daughter? You going to try to fix that situation?"

"I will. Someday."

"And there's a man somewhere, I'd guess. Maybe that little girl's father."

"There's a man, but not her father."

"Someone you have a future with, though."

"I hope so."

"There you go," he said. "What else can you ask for? Sometimes God hands you gifts, and you have to hold on to them with everything you've got, or lose them forever. It took me a long time to learn that."

He stood. "But enough preaching. I'm wiped out. I'm going to try to get some sleep."

He looked down at the bag.

"Take it in with you, if it'll make you feel better," she said. "I won't be offended."

He exhaled, then shook his head. "I guess it's safe out here. If you wanted the whole thing, I never would have gotten back here alive anyway, right?"

"That's right."

"Try to get some sleep yourself. You look like you could use it." He went into the bedroom, closed the door softly behind him.

She brought the bottle in from the kitchen, refilled the glass, went to the radio and turned it on low. It was still set to QXR. Something calming and quiet she didn't recognize. Mozart maybe. Brahms.

She sat back on the couch, drank wine, looked at the bedroom door. This is your celebration, she thought. Drinking alone. Remembering the faces of a man and woman seconds before their lives ended, their blood on the bag at your feet. There wasn't enough wine in the bottle to block that out. There wasn't enough wine in the world.

She stretched out on the couch, too tired to get a pillow or blanket from the closet. She pulled her duffel bag closer, set the Glock atop it, in easy reach.

She drank wine, looked up at the ceiling, letting the music take her. She closed her eyes.

# NINETEEN

She woke all at once, with a moment of panic, not knowing where she was. The Glock was in her hand. She looked down at the duffel bag, and it all came back to her.

Benny was standing in the bedroom doorway. He had his coat on. Marta was behind him.

"We were thinking we'd get going," he said.

She set the Glock back on the duffel, sat up. "What time is it?"

"Three o'clock."

More than twelve hours since she'd gone up that hill. Only four hours' sleep. Her hips ached, and her neck was sore. The bottle on the table was half empty.

"Stay right there," she said. She went into the bathroom, ran the faucet, palmed water in her face, drank some and spit it out. Her mouth was dry, her lips chapped.

"Marta and I decided the best thing to do would be to get on the move," he said. "Put in as many miles as we can today."

She wiped her face with a towel, looked at him. They'd brought their suitcases into the living room. "What's your plan?"

"We'll take the Honda, if that's okay with you. We'll leave it at a train station, airport maybe, call you and tell you where it is."

She nodded at the duffel. "You think you're going to get that on a plane?"

"No. Safer on a train. Not sure where we're headed yet. We'll figure that out on the way. I want to get clear of here, though."

"Good idea."

"What about you?"

"I've got some things to do first."

"I'm worried about all this coming back on you."

"Don't. I can take care of myself."

"Yeah, I've seen."

He looked around the living room, then back at her. "Then I guess this is it."

"It is."

"Thanks for looking out for us. Thanks for everything."

Marta said, "Benny, we should go."

He lifted the duffel. "Heavier than I thought it'd be."

"Way it is sometimes," Crissa said.

"I don't imagine we'll be coming back this way, for any reason," Benny said. "Maybe ever."

"Don't."

"Give my regards to Jimmy. Thank him for me."

"I will."

Marta said, "Benny." She had the suitcases.

He hefted the duffel, the carry strap over his shoulder. Crissa went past them to the door, unlocked and opened it. The Honda and the Taurus were parked on the concrete apron outside.

"Good luck," she said.

"Thanks." He stopped at the door, put out his hand. She took it.

"I wish I'd known you thirty years ago," he said. "We could have run our own crew. No one could have touched us."

"I don't want to run anything," she said. "Never did."

"Benny, we need to go," Marta said.

"Be safe," Crissa said. "And be careful with that money."

"I will," he said.

She watched them load the car, back out. As they pulled away, Benny powered down his window, put out a hand, raised it high.

Back inside, she made coffee, took the cup out on the deck. The sky was clear, no clouds in sight. A charter fishing boat chugged up the inlet, headed for open water. Water slapped against the bulkhead as it went past.

She'd sit out here for a while, finish her coffee, then do what had to be done. First she'd call Anthony Falcone, tell him what she had for his grandfather. Then Rathka, to ask him what he thought she should do with a million dollars in cash.

They got on the Garden State Parkway, headed north. He was exhausted from the night before, but wanted to keep moving. They'd decided to drive to New Haven tonight, leave the car at the Amtrak station, pick a train. Head south maybe, live in a hotel for a while, figure out what to do next.

Crossing the Driscoll Bridge, he saw the first signs for Staten Island. He chewed a lip.

"What's wrong?" she said.

He shook his head. Keep going, he thought. Get clear of here. Run. It's what you do best.

"There's a service area coming up," he said. "I'm going to stop."

"Why?"

"There's something I need to do."

"What?"

"Something important."

He signaled, guided the Honda into the lot.

"We shouldn't be doing this, Benny. We should be getting away from here."

"We will," he said.

He backed into a spot on the far side of the parking area, near a grove of trees.

"What's this about?"

"It won't take long, I promise."

There was a gift shop in the plaza, and he found what he wanted—a cheap, green zippered tote bag that read NEW JERSEY AND YOU: PERFECT TOGETHER in yellow type against a silhouette of the state.

He carried it back to the Honda, opened the trunk. With the woods at his back, he unzipped the duffel, counted out $75,000 in packs of hundreds. She got out of the car, watched him.

The money filled the overnight bag. He zipped it shut, slung it over his shoulder, closed the trunk lid.

"What's that for?" she said.

"A debt," he said. "One I've owed for a long time."


He called Hersh twice from the car, but there was no answer at the house or the shop. He realized he hadn't spoken to him since that first day back in Brooklyn. It felt like a lifetime ago.

He tried the house again, let it ring seven times. No machine. He hung up.

"What's wrong?" she said.

"I'm trying to reach Hersh, but the shop's closed and no one's home."

"Call his cell."

"I don't have the number. I doubt he even has one. We'll have to drive out there anyway. My bet is he's holed up in the shop, doing his books, not answering the phone. He's like that."

"Is that who the money's for?"

"Some of it. Mostly it's for Ethan and Lena, when he sees them."

"How do you know he won't just keep it?"

"He won't. Hersh and I never agreed on much, but he was always stand-up. Too honest for his own good."

"What's that mean?"

"Sometimes you have to go along to get along," he said. "You can swim against the tide, but sooner or later it pulls you under."

"That what you did, 'Go along to get along'?"

"All my life," he said.

The shop was dark, the CLOSED sign in the window. He tried the door, then leaned on the service bell, heard it ring deep inside. Marta watched from the car. He'd double-parked, left the hazards on.

He rang the bell again, used a hand to block the glare, peered through the glass. No movement inside.

He went back to the car, shook his head. When he got in, she said, "What do we do?"

"His place is only a few blocks away. We'll try there, and I'll give him another call. If he's not home, I'll have to figure out something else."

"We can't come back here after this. Even to give someone money, family or not."

"I know," he said. "Why I want to do it now, get it over with."

Hersh's street was tree-lined, old brownstones and redbrick town houses. They had to circle the block twice before they found a parking spot on the cross street, next to an ivy-covered church wall.

"Wait here," he said. He reached into the backseat, got the tote bag.

"I should come with you."

"Better to wait. If he's not there, I'll be back in a couple minutes. If he is, we'll want to talk a little."

"And that's none of my business?"

"I didn't say that."

"Go on," she said. "I'll wait here. So nobody steals the car."

"Baby, compared to some parts of Brooklyn, this is Beverly Hills."

"I've never been there, either."

"Someday I'll take you," he said. He leaned over, kissed her cheek. "That's a promise."

He got out, walked down the tree-shaded street, the sun sinking behind the long row of houses.

Hersh's was midblock, a two-level redbrick with a small front yard. Benny went up the steps, rang the bell, waited, then knocked hard. No response. He got out his cell, called the house number again. He could hear the ringing inside.

A bus nosed to the curb. Benny turned. The door hissed open, and an old woman with a walker got off, crossed the street, didn't look at him. The bus pulled away.

He rang the bell again, thought he heard movement inside. Then silence once more.

Turn around, he thought. Go back to the car, to Marta. Call

Hersh from wherever you end up, figure out a way to get the money to him then. Worry about it later. Walk away now.

He leaned off the steps to look through the gap in the front curtains. The living room was empty. He heard the sound again then, something like a groan.

Maybe he's hurt in there, Benny thought. Diabetic shock. A stroke. His heart. You can't just leave. If you owe him anything, you owe him that much.

He went back down the steps, and into the narrow alley that ran alongside the house. The backyard had a chain-link fence, almost solid with ivy, the gate open. Nearly dark now, the yard was black with shadow. He went in, saw the back door ajar, darkness inside.

"Hersh?" he called out. "Hersh, you in there?"

When there was no answer, he went up the two steps, nudged the door wider with the tote bag. "Hersh?"

The muffled groan came again, from somewhere deep in the house. It was then he saw the splintered wood in the door frame.

He backed down the steps, heard movement behind him, started to turn. Cold metal touched the back of his neck.

"Give me an excuse," Perry said.

When Benny didn't move, Perry pushed him toward the door. "Inside, rat."

Benny went up and into the kitchen. Perry shoved him again, and Hersh was there in the living room, in a straight-back chair, gagged, hands bound behind him. He looked more angry than scared.

Across from him, Sal Bruno sat on the couch. He looked at Benny without speaking. On the coffee table in front of him were a leather slapjack and a straight razor. A single lamp lit the room.

"Man," Perry said. "Did you fuck up big this time."

# TWENTY

When Rathka came on the line, Crissa said, "Good news, bad news." She was in the living room, the money lined up in stacks on the coffee table. Jimmy's fifty grand was in a brown Whole Foods bag at her feet.

"Bad news first," he said. "Always."

"I need to get away from here for a while. Head south maybe."

"When?"

"Tomorrow, if I can swing it. If not, the next day. I have a couple things to do first, then I'll catch a train."

"Heat?"

"Not that kind. Just being careful."

"As always."

"I want to hold on to this place, though. I'll be back at some point, before long. I'll pay another three months up front to keep it off the market."

"I'm sure we can make that work."

"I was thinking I might go down to Kenedy, stay nearby. I'd like to be there when our friend walks out the gate."

"Okay. What's the good news?"

"I have a significant amount of capital to invest."

"How significant?"

"Seven figures."

"Raw?"

"Raw, but cold. It's been out of circulation for a while. I have to take some off the top, then I need a strategy for the rest. I'll need regular access to part of it, the rest I want to put away."

"Any ideas?"

"I want to set up another account for Maddie, in the islands maybe. Something that's not so closely monitored, where I can make deposits without anyone wondering where they came from."

"I'll get on it. You must trust your cousin."

"I do. Later, when we're settled, I'll want to take another look at that arrangement. I'll pay Leah a visit when I'm down there."

"I put in the request for a call, but scheduling's been an issue."

"How's that?"

"I thought they were just dragging their feet at first, institutional red tape. But apparently our friend's the holdup. He doesn't want to talk to me."

"Why?"

"I don't know. Our guard down there doesn't know, either, but he confirms the reason. Hearing's set for noon next Wednesday, but it could be delayed. God knows it's been before. But there's nothing we can do about that."

"I'll be down there, just in case."

"You sound different. Something in your voice. Things are going better, I guess."

"My luck changed," she said. "Not sure how long it will last, so I want to run with it while it's good."

"Glad to hear. But if you want to make a deposit, especially one of that size, we should find some neutral ground. Here isn't so good right now."

"I'll work it out and let you know," she said. "I'm ditching this cell soon. I'll call you when I have a new one. We'll find some place to meet."

"Looking forward to it," he said. She ended the call.

Perry took the tote bag from Benny's hand. He had a bruise on his forehead, his eyes dark with fatigue. "This what I hope it is?"

"Give that here," Sal said. Perry tossed the bag to him. Sal unzipped it, looked inside. Hersh was watching all of them. He'd been gagged with a dish towel that was wound tight, tied behind his head. His lip was split, and there were spots of blood on his white shirt.

"On your knees, slick," Perry said. When Benny didn't move, Perry kicked him in the back of the knee. Benny's leg went out from under him. He landed on his side.

Sal looked through the money. "How much is this?"

Benny rose to his knees, looked at Hersh, said, "I'm sorry."

"Don't worry about him," Perry said. "Worry about me." He had a blue-steel automatic in his hand. "Answer the man."

Benny looked at Sal. "Seventy-five grand."

Sal, expressionless, said, "Where's the rest?"

"I don't have it."

Sal zipped the bag back up, set it on the floor. He took a cell from his jacket pocket, opened it, dialed a number.

"Yeah, Danny," he said. "You were right. He showed up." He

listened, said, "No, just him." Another pause. "Okay. Let me call you back." He closed the phone, put it away.

To Perry, he said, "Danny says go look for the car, it's got to be nearby. Maybe the others are there, too. Be careful."

Perry nodded at Benny. "What about this one?"

"I'll watch him. He's not going anywhere."

Perry stuck the gun in his belt, zipped his jacket up to cover it, went into the kitchen, and out the back door. Benny hoped Marta would see him coming, drive away, not come back. But it wouldn't work like that, he knew. She wouldn't leave him.

Sal got up with a sigh, stepped behind Hersh and untied the towel. He tossed it aside. Hersh coughed, spit.

"He had nothing to do with any of this," Benny said. "He didn't even know where I was."

"That's what he was saying," Sal said. "I was just going to get started on him when you came along. Saved us the trouble."

Hersh craned his neck, trying to see Sal behind him.

"Way it looks, though," Sal said, "is that you're dropping off his cut."

"I wouldn't take a dime from him, for anything," Hersh said. He coughed again. "I don't know anything about that money. Ask *him* where it came from."

"I know where it came from," Sal said. He took a snub-nosed revolver from his belt, broke open the cylinder, looked at the shells, then clicked it shut, put the gun back in his belt.

Hersh looked at Benny. "I always knew it would come to this. You destroy everything around you, don't you? Like a disease. You don't care who pays the price, as long as you get what you want."

"I'm sorry, Hersh." He looked at Sal. "All this is my fault. It has nothing to do with anyone else."

"Listen to the man," Hersh said. "He's telling the truth."

Noises in the kitchen, then Perry came through, pushing Marta ahead of him, her arm twisted behind her. He had the duffel slung over his left shoulder.

Benny closed his eyes, opened them again. What have I done? he thought. We were almost out of here, clear. How did I screw this up so bad again?

"Benny." She tried to go to him, and Perry dragged her back, propelled her toward the couch. "Sit your sweet ass down."

He dropped the duffel on the floor, said, "Check that shit out."

Sal said, "You look inside?"

"Yeah, not the whole nut, but a lot of it. Maybe half. What are we gonna do?"

"Half's not good enough. Danny says we should take them up to the Victory. You still got those plastic things?"

"Yeah," Perry said.

Marta was sitting up now, her eyes moving from Benny to Hersh to the others, her face pale.

Benny could feel his heart beating in his chest, the pulse of blood in his neck. Perry stepped behind him, said, "Hands."

Benny didn't move. Perry put the gun to the back of his head. "Hands, slick. Or your brains are all over this nice carpet."

Benny crossed his arms behind him. Perry put away the gun, grabbed his wrists, wrapped a flex-cuff around them, cinched it tight. Benny winced at the pain.

"I've got nothing to do with any of that money," Hersh said. "I swear. Tell them, Benny."

"Do I look like I give a shit?" Sal said.

Benny saw Marta looking at the front door. If she ran, kept going, she might make it. He could throw himself at Sal, tangle them up long enough that she could be clear and away. As long as she didn't look back.

216 | Wallace Stroby

To Sal, he said, "Take the money. Take it all. Keep it, the two of you. Tell Danny we got away. He'll never know the truth. There's a million dollars in there. You two can split it. How much will you get bringing it back to Danny?"

Marta cut a glance at him. He nodded slightly, tensed, got ready to stand, make his run at Sal.

"Well, that's something to think about, isn't it?" Perry said. "But you must not know Danny very well, think anybody could get away with that shit with him."

"I know him well enough," Benny said, wanting to keep them talking, distracted. "I could tell you stories about Danny. Anybody ever tell you about the time that . . ."

Marta bolted from the couch. Benny tried to stand, but his legs were numb, nerveless. Perry caught her arm, spun her around, dropped her. She grunted when she hit the carpet. He pinned her there, facedown.

Benny felt Sal grab his jacket, pull him off balance and to the side. Perry pressed Marta down, took another flex-cuff from his jacket pocket, wound it around her wrists. She tried to buck him off, and he laughed, pressed his crotch into her jeans.

"A fighter," he said. "I like that. Gets me hard." He locked the cuff, climbed off her.

"Enough of this shit," Sal said. "I'm tired. Let's get out of here." He took out the snub-nose.

"Tough guys, is that what you are?" Hersh said. "Beating up on women and old men?"

"What was that?" Sal said.

Benny got to his knees again, felt a stone of pressure in his chest.

Hersh tried to pull his shoulders back, a semblance of dignity. "For years, we had to live with your type. Corrupting everything you touched. Taking money from working people, destroying lives, putting drugs on the street. You're a blight on the earth." He spit on the floor. *"Gonif. Khazer."*

"You're a tough old Jew, aren't you?" Sal said. "Don't take shit from anyone."

"Not from scum like you."

"Hersh, shut up," Benny said. Marta had twisted on the floor to watch them.

Hersh spit again, said, *"Faygeleh."*

"I have no idea what that means," Sal said, and shot him twice in the chest.

Marta cried out. Benny closed his eyes. The sound of the shots echoed through the house.

"Maybe Hitler had the right idea," Sal said.

Benny opened his eyes. There was a haze of cordite smoke in front of him. Hersh was slumped motionless, eyes half open, the front of his shirt slowly turning red. Marta began to sob.

"There you go," Sal said. "End of discussion."

"Jesus Christ," Perry said. "There's people live around here, Sal. That was loud. We need to roll."

Sal put the gun back in his belt. "Gag these two, then bring the Explorer around front. We'll put them in the back. Find a blanket or something to cover them. I'll take the money."

Perry was looking at the duffel bag.

"Forget it," Sal said. "We're bringing it to Danny. You'll get your cut later, with everyone else. When we've got all of it."

"That's okay," Perry said. "I can wait."

# TWENTY-ONE

By 10:00 P.M., Crissa had all her money packed into two new suitcases. The duffel would go into a dumpster in another town. She'd sleep at a motel tonight, take Jimmy his money in the morning, then call Rathka. With Benny and Marta gone, there was no reason to stay here. He was right. It would be better to be on the move, safer. She'd say her good-byes for now, then get ready for Texas.

When her cell rang, she looked at the number, saw it was Benny's. Calling about the car.

"Yeah," she answered. "Where is it?"

Silence, then a hoarse voice said, "That's what I was going to ask you."

She waited, said nothing.

"Where are you?" Taliferro said. "Probably far away from here now, right? That was some stunt with the Escalade. Twice now you fucked things up for me."

"What do you want?"

"What do you think?"

"I think you're out of luck."

"It's your partner here who's out of luck."

"I don't have one."

"That's too bad. Because if that's the case, he's going to die for nothing. His squeeze, too. And I guarantee it won't be easy for either of them."

Stupid, she thought. They should have been on their way and gone. Safe. Unless Benny had stopped somewhere, done something he shouldn't.

"You listening?" Taliferro said.

She let out her breath. "I'm listening."

"What do you have to say?"

"Do what you have to do."

"It's like that? And here all the time he was trying to protect you."

Hang up, she thought. Toss the phone, cut your ties. What Benny got into was his own fault. There was nothing for it.

"You're still there?" Taliferro said.

"Yeah, I'm still here."

"Good. Because let me make one thing clear to you. I don't know who the fuck you are, and I don't care. But that money you've got? It's mine. You stole it from me, and nobody steals from me, ever, and gets away with it. That's what Benny found out. What you will, too."

"If I know you, he's dead already."

"No, not yet. And you don't know me at all. Don't even imagine you do."

"I'm hanging up," she said.

"Don't do that. You think this is over? Even if you get away now, sooner or later your name's gonna come up. Somebody'll mention a female heister, worked out of Jersey, and that's all it'll take. And then we'll find you. I guarantee that."

She felt sourness in her stomach, the beginning of pain there. He was right. They'd keep looking. Eventually the search would lead them to Jimmy and Anthony. If anything happened to them, it would be on her.

"What?" he said. "You think I'm bluffing about all this? You think I'm not standing in a room right now with both of them?" Then, to someone else, "Bring the girl over here. Give me that razor."

Crissa's stomach tightened.

"Yeah," Taliferro said. "Hold her there."

Muffled noises, then the sound of a slap. Crissa gripped the phone.

"Hear this?" he said. He tapped something against the receiver. "It's a straight razor. She's been doing pretty good so far, a little banged up, but nothing serious, nothing permanent."

"It doesn't matter. She doesn't mean anything to me."

"No? You should see her. She's been trying to tough it out so far. But we'll see how tough she is when I start on her face. She won't be so pretty with her ears gone."

"That the kind of thing gets you off?"

"Not so much anymore. Not as much as you showing up here with a duffel bag full of my money."

"You'll kill them anyway."

"Him, maybe. I have a score to settle. But her? Why do that? You turn over that money, I'll let you both walk. Maybe Benny, too, after we teach him a lesson. It's up to you."

"I'm supposed to believe that?"

"Believe what you want. Best thing about this place we are right now? They can scream as loud and as long as they want, and nobody's going to hear them. I know that for a fact."

"I can't help you."

"Then whatever happens, it's your fault. Remember that. These boys are getting a little itchy, impatient. I've held them back a couple times, but I don't think I can do it anymore. If they want to pull a train on her, who am I to tell them no? Long as they use condoms, so there's no DNA when someone finds whatever's left of her, right?"

The pain in her stomach was like a pebble of fire now. "Where are you?"

"That's better. Here's the deal, and it's a one-time-only thing. You bring me the rest of that money. If it's all there—and there's no surprises—I let the girl go."

"What about Roth?"

"I have to think about that. You know where the Victory is?"

"What's that?"

"I guess you wouldn't. It's Brooklyn. Canarsie. You call me on this phone when you get over the Verrazano. I'll tell you where to go."

"I'm nowhere near there."

"Then you better get moving. Like I said, it's a one-shot deal. By tomorrow this whole thing is over, one way or another."

"What time?"

"Let's say midnight. That way, we start the new day fresh, right? All this behind us."

"Not enough time."

"That's too bad," he said. "Because it's all the time you've got."

# TWENTY-TWO

Benny lay on cold tile, hands bound behind him, and watched a roach crawl slowly up the wall. The room smelled of mold and urine. Behind him, he heard the steady drip of water in the ancient sink. Marta lay across the room, bound and gagged, facing him. Behind her was a claw-foot bathtub, a plastic shower curtain drawn across it, dark with mildew. Her eyes were closed, tears leaking out.

I'm sorry, baby, he thought. I'm sorry about everything.

The man named Dominic came into the room, balancing on crutches. He stuck a tip into Benny's stomach. "Hey, remember me, old man?"

Benny looked up at him. His glasses were crooked, the left lens blurry.

"Yeah, it's me," Dominic said. He jabbed the tip at Benny's face, forced him to pull his head back. "Look at you now, huh?"

Taliferro came into the room with Sal. "Dom, give us a couple minutes here. Go downstairs with the others. I'll be down in a few." Dominic nodded, hobbled out into the hallway.

Taliferro took out a handkerchief, used it to lower the toilet seat, then spread it over the lid before he sat down.

"There's a way you can make this easier," he said. "For both of you."

Sal pulled the shower curtain away from the tub, reached in. Benny heard a faucet squeal. Pipes banged, and then water spurted out, clotted with air at first, then a steady stream. Sal watched it for a moment, then shut it back off. "It'll do." He left the room.

Benny looked up at Taliferro, blinked. Taliferro leaned forward and straightened his glasses, pushed them farther up on his nose. "There. That better?"

Benny could see more clearly now, the room in focus. There was a pebbled window behind the tub, moonlight coming in. Marta's eyes were open now. She was watching them, not crying anymore.

"You know, we could have been partners in all this," Taliferro said. "When I first tracked you down. We could have gone into this together, worked it all out."

Benny swallowed, felt vomit rising, fought it back down.

"No hard feelings, though," Taliferro said. He rubbed his shoulder. "This is still sore, you know that? You got me good. But we need to move on, right? Who knows, this might be our last chance to talk."

"If I'd led you to the money," Benny said, "you would have killed me anyway, as soon as you had it."

"Maybe. Maybe not. We got lucky with the Scalise woman. I knew Joey had been banging her, but I didn't think he'd leave her all that cash. Pussy-whipped, I guess. Wasn't hard to track her down. I sent Perry up there to keep an eye on her, just in case. Same way I sent him and Sal to your brother-in-law's. Just in case. Worked out both times, huh?"

"He didn't have to kill Hersh."

"Once he got to that point, what was he gonna do? He didn't have a choice. But that's your fault, Benny. No one else's."

Benny twisted his wrists, trying to get feeling back into his fingers. The flex-cuff cut deeper into his skin.

"Like I said, we got lucky with that woman. While we were wasting time chasing your sorry ass, she had it all the while. Perry watched her for a few days, saw her moving money out. Then we made our move. Probably same thing you did, right?"

Sal came back in, carrying a dark green toolbox. He set it atop the sink, opened the clasps.

"Hold off on that," Taliferro said. "We're going to talk some more first."

"Okay. I'll get the suitcases ready."

When he was gone, Taliferro said, "All that trouble you put us through, and see where you ended up anyway? Back in Brooklyn. Full circle. But the end of the line this time." He pointed a thumb at Marta. "For her, too. And that's a shame. It didn't have to be that way."

"Kill me if you have to," Benny said, "but let her go. She wasn't involved in any of this. She won't say anything to anybody."

"We're past that now, though, aren't we? I mean, let's be men here, face facts. You fucked up and this is where it got you. Both of you."

Benny closed his eyes, felt the familiar pressure in his chest. Willing it this time to expand, fill him, blot out what was happening. End it all now. But Marta . . .

He opened his eyes, looked across at her. She met his gaze. She was dry-eyed now, past fear and into something else.

"If you want this to go easier, then you need to tell me some things," Taliferro said. "You need to tell me who that woman is, how you met her, where she is now."

"I don't know."

"You have any idea how pissed off this made me? All of us? It should have been easy with Joey's girlfriend. It *was* easy. She showed us the safe in the basement—a big one—and gave up the combination so quick you wouldn't believe it. And then you and that broad had to come and fuck everything up. Almost put us all in the hospital."

"I'm sorry."

"I'm not saying you'll get out of this alive, because you won't. But the girl, maybe she has a chance. Depending on what you tell us."

"You've got that money. There's a million dollars in there, just take it."

"Why would I settle for one million when I can have two?"

"That woman's long gone now. I don't know where. Take the money, it's yours. Just let Marta go."

"I know it's mine. It's *been* mine. Who the fuck are you to tell me that? You're giving it to me, that what you think? It's your gift to me?"

"Danny, please."

"What's the woman's name?"

Benny swallowed, drew in breath. The pain had settled somewhere in the middle of his chest. He could hear voices downstairs, laughter.

"I only know the one she gave me. It's probably phony."

"What was it?"

He pulled it from the air. "Sarah."

"Sarah what?"

"Edwards."

"Bullshit."

"It's the name she gave me. That's all I know."

"How'd you hook up with her?"

"I met her at the Galaxy, on Lefferts Boulevard. That's where she hung out. Some guy there told me about her." Taking a chance with it, wondering if he'd gone too far.

Taliferro frowned. "You are one lying fuck, you know that? And here I thought we were having a serious conversation. If there was a female heister working out of the Galaxy, don't you think I'd know about it?"

"That's where I met her, I swear."

"Who introduced you?"

"The bartender there. I don't know his name. I told him I was a friend of Leo Bloomgold."

Taliferro looked at him. Wondering if it was true, Benny thought. Maybe halfway buying it already.

Taliferro shook his head, called out, "Perry." Footsteps on the stairs, and then Perry came into the bathroom. "Yeah, skip?"

"Take the girl in the bedroom."

"About time."

"Just leave her there for now. Don't touch her until I say so."

"I can wait," Perry said. He grabbed her by the arm, hauled her up. "Come on, sugar tits." She groaned beneath the gag, and Benny could see the pain in her face. He closed his eyes, heard Perry walk her out, her step unsteady.

"What happens next is your choice," Taliferro said. Benny opened his eyes. They were burning. His stomach felt hollow and empty.

"Please, Danny. I'm begging you."

"What I don't understand, you've been a rat your whole life, why clam up now?"

"I've told you everything I know."

Taliferro looked at his watch. "Eleven thirty. What are the chances she actually shows up?"

Benny didn't answer.

"I'd say slim to none," Taliferro said. "She's got half the money, why would she care what happens to you? But I'll find her eventually. What else can you tell me about her?"

Benny closed his eyes again, shook his head slowly.

"Think about it," Taliferro said. "You tell me everything you know, I make it quick for you, and we let the girl go. You don't talk, it gets ugly."

Benny kept his eyes closed.

"*Pratico,*" Taliferro said. "Like a mule you are. Your Marta know anything about this woman? Maybe she's got something to tell us?"

Benny opened his eyes. "She doesn't know anything."

"Then you're not leaving me with much, are you?" He reached into his coat pocket, took out Benny's cell phone, squinted at it. "She was supposed to call when she came over the bridge, so I could tell her how to get here. Didn't think she'd go for it, but what the hell? Worth a shot, at least."

He set the phone on the sink.

"So if she's not coming," he said, "then that just leaves me and you, doesn't it?"

This part of Brooklyn was all dark warehouses and shuttered businesses, no houses in sight. For a while, Crissa had driven with dark water to her right, moonlight glinting off the surface, the lights of the Verrazano in her rearview. Now she passed a long stretch of wetlands, an illuminated sign that read FOUNTAIN

AVENUE RECLAMATION PROJECT. She wore the windbreaker, a black sweater, dark sneakers. The Glock was under the seat.

Five minutes and three wrong turns later, she found one of the cross streets she'd been watching for. It took her across abandoned train tracks and deeper into an industrial area. Brake shops and tire stores, truck garages with razor-wire lots, everything shut up tight.

She'd mapped out the location of the Victory Lounge online, knew she ran a risk by not calling. Taliferro might get tired of waiting, and kill them both. But there was nothing she could do about that now.

When she was near the block, she shut off the headlights, steered the Taurus onto a side street. She parked alongside a long, windowless building, killed the engine. Scattered streetlights, no other cars around.

The moon was full and high, a white disc in the clouds. Threshold moment, she thought. Turn around now, go back and get your share of the money, head south. Or see this through, however it ends up.

She knew what Wayne would tell her. *You've got the money, Red. That's what you went into it for. That's what it's all about, why you risked your life. Nothing else matters.*

But Taliferro was right. If she left, it would never be over.

She took out the Glock, eased the slide back, checked the round. The .32 was in her right front jeans pocket. In the left was the extra magazine for the Glock.

She put the Glock in her jacket pocket, pried loose the plastic cover from the overhead courtesy light, popped out the bulbs. Then she got out of the car, and moved into the shadows.

# TWENTY-THREE

Benny was shaking. The chill that came up through the tile floor had settled in his muscles and joints. His hands were numb from the flex-cuffs.

Sal leaned in the doorway, and said, "How long we gonna wait?"

"A little bit longer," Taliferro said. He looked at his watch. "Just midnight now, so we'll give it a little while. Just in case we need to put him on the phone."

"Should I get the rest of my stuff?"

"Might as well." Sal went out.

Taliferro looked down at Benny. "You remember this place? You know what it is?"

"I know."

"I shut it down a few years ago. Now it's like a private club. I use it for shape-ups, keep everybody in line. Everything's still here, though—jukebox, pool table. I keep the bar stocked. Gives the guys a place to socialize, stay out of trouble. And there's a bedroom up here if they need one. That's where your girlfriend is."

Benny opened and closed his hands, felt pin and needles in his fingers, the blood starting to flow back into them.

"Patsy bought this place back in the seventies," Taliferro said. "It used to be full of wiseguys all the time. All the crews came here to drink, to bullshit. Jimmy the Gent, everybody. Never Joey D, though. He was too good for us, didn't want to mix with the help, you know? You were around back then, Benny. You remember what it was like."

Benny's mouth was dry. "I remember."

"We used to run this city. You wanted to get anything done, especially in Brooklyn or Queens, you came to us. We owned the politicians. The cops, too. You didn't have to worry about anything. The niggers, the spic gangs, they all respected us, knew who was boss. Nobody fucked with us. It's not like that anymore, let me tell you. Everything's gone to hell."

"What are you going to do? If she doesn't call?"

"You in a rush to find out?"

Benny didn't answer.

"Aren't many of us old-timers left," Taliferro said. "You and me, we got that in common, even if you did turn out to be a rat. These young guys, they're good, but you can't explain it to them, the way it was. Sal was around then, so he knows. He was just a kid, but he could get things done."

Taliferro took out a pack of Marlboros and the silver lighter, lit a cigarette. "If these walls could talk, right?" He blew smoke out. "Some shit took place in here, let me tell you. You got invited up here, there was no telling what was going to happen. Made guys—tough guys—they'd be shaking in their boots, crapping themselves, if they thought Patsy was mad at them. Sometimes we'd be downstairs, drinking, playing the jukebox, and some poor bastard would be up here getting his balls cut off. We never heard a thing."

Sal came in, dropped a bundle on the floor, flipped it open with his foot. Green plastic sheeting.

Sal looked at Benny, then at the tub. "I may need a hand getting him over there."

In the doorway, Perry said, "Frankie just called from outside. Says no sign of anybody. No cars driving by, nothing."

"Then that's that," Taliferro said. He looked at his watch again. "Almost twelve thirty. No reason to keep waiting, I guess."

Sal took the straight razor from his pocket, set it on the sink. He opened the toolbox.

Benny twisted to look behind him. The cracked mirror reflected the contents of the box—a hacksaw with a plastic handle, two butcher knives, garden shears.

He felt his bladder weaken. A warm wetness crept down his right thigh.

Taliferro looked at the toolbox, and said, "Haven't seen those in a while."

"All new," Sal said. "Sharp. Shouldn't be a problem."

Perry swallowed. "I don't know if I'm down with this."

"You don't have to be," Sal said. "I got it. I just need you to help me get him over there, then hold him still while I cut him. Then we just let him drain out."

"How long's that take?"

Sal shrugged. "Forty-five minutes maybe. An hour, if we want to be sure."

Perry looked at Taliferro. "What about the girl?"

"We'll hold off a little bit on that," Taliferro said. "We may need her. Don't worry. You'll get your shot before we're done with her."

He turned back to Benny. "Sounds like your partner abandoned you. No need to protect her anymore then, is there? It's not too late to make this thing easier, you know. For you and the girl both."

Benny closed his eyes. He could give them the name she'd used, but knew it wouldn't change what was going to happen. They wouldn't let Marta go, no matter what he told them.

This is what it's all come to, he thought. After all this time, all his running, this was the way it had ended up, for both of them. Hot tears came to his eyes.

She stood on the flat roof of a truck garage, looked at the building across the street. Two stories, redbrick. The second-floor windows were plywooded over, but edges of light shone around three of them.

The street entrance was a black door, dark windows on either side. Through the glass, she could see the faint glow of light inside. A torn awning read ORY LOUN E, the letters faded.

It was a corner building. On the left side, a fire escape ran up to the roof. On the right, an empty lot—overgrown grass, broken cinder blocks, a shopping cart on its side. The rest of the block was dark and silent. Storefronts with metal gates, graffiti scrawled across them. Low-roofed garages and warehouses. A single street lamp lit half the block. Two others were dark, burned out.

Two vehicles were parked on the side street. A dark blue Ford Explorer, and the Lincoln Town Car she'd seen in Staten Island. There would be no way to tell how many men were inside the building, until it was too late.

She looked at the boarded-up windows, remembered what Benny had told her. People went in there, but never came out.

In the distance, the lights of the Verrazano. The moon hung above it, illuminating the clouds.

They don't know you're here, she thought. You could go back to the car, leave now. What Benny would do if the situation were reversed.

A burning knot seemed to grow in her stomach. She looked at her watch: twelve thirty. He and the girl might be dead inside there already, probably were. If they were ever there in the first place.

Taliferro stood, stretched and yawned, hands in the small of his back. He flicked the cigarette into the sink. It landed hissing.

Sal was leaning against the wall, arms folded, Perry in the doorway behind him.

"What's going on out there?" Taliferro said.

"Nothing," Perry said.

"Okay, tell Frankie to bring the money up. We'll count it a final time, do the split here. Get it over with."

When he left, Taliferro looked at Sal. "You ready for this?"

"I'm ready."

"Gonna be a long night."

Sal shrugged.

Crissa crossed the street a block away, staying close to the buildings. On the opposite corner, she waited in a doorway, watching.

Faint light under the awning, someone opening a cell phone, a bandage over his eye. Frankie Longo. She hadn't seen him, hadn't known anyone was there.

Careless. She should have known they'd post someone outside.

She'd almost blundered into his sightline, raised the alarm before she was ready.

She waited. He spoke into the phone, then closed it, opened the black door, went inside.

She counted off three minutes, and when no one came back out, she crossed the street in shadow.

Benny watched as Perry and Longo carried the duffel in between them. They dropped it near his legs.

"He piss himself?" Longo said.

"Can you blame him?" Taliferro said.

"Guess not."

"Dominic still downstairs?"

"Yeah," Longo said. "He's keeping an eye on the street."

"Good. The money from the bag, that go back in with the rest?"

"It's all in there," Perry said.

"Let's count it out one last time," Taliferro said. "Then divide it up."

"You don't have to tell me twice," Longo said. He knelt, unzipped the duffel.

"You've got the money," Benny said. "What good is killing us going to do?"

"This guy never gives up," Sal said.

"Don't do this," Benny said. "Please don't."

"You had your chance to talk," Taliferro said. "That time's over. Don't beg. Don't demean yourself. It won't change anything."

"Danny, I'm sorry. The shit I did, that was me. It had nothing to do with Marta."

"Bad luck for her then, isn't it? Getting mixed up with you."

"This isn't right."

"'Right,'" Taliferro said, "has got nothing to do with anything."

# TWENTY-FOUR

There was a metal trash can near the rear of the building. She dragged it over to the fire escape, overturned it, climbed up. From there, she could reach the bottom rung of the ladder.

The can started to buckle under her, but she had a good grip now. She stepped off, dragged the last section of fire escape down with her, hinges creaking. Flakes of rust rained down.

She went up slowly. The second-floor window was boarded. She could hear muffled voices inside, but couldn't make out the words. She moved on up to the roof.

The surface here was tar and tin flashing, spotted with pigeon droppings. It creaked under her. In the moonlight, she could see the roof door, the padlock there. She could hear the distant hum of traffic on the Belt Parkway.

She stepped carefully, testing for weak spots. When she reached the door, she got out the penlight, shone it on the latch. It was an elongated padlock, but an old one. She looked around, saw a discarded bit of flashing a few feet away. She carried it over, took out her pocket knife, and used the tip of the blade to carve a ragged *M* shape in the thin metal, an inch across.

She put the penlight away; the moon was bright enough to work by. She folded the metal *M* over on itself, slid it around the locking bar of the padlock, forced it down into the mechanism. She jiggled it until she felt the metal teeth engage the tumblers. The lock popped open. She took it off the latch, set it down on the roof.

The door creaked loudly when she tried it. She drew the Glock with her right hand, pulled at the door handle with her left. The hinges were stiff, and she had to jerk the door to get it open. Bits of rotten wood fell away from the jamb. She pointed the Glock in. A short flight of unlit stairs, then an open doorway and a corridor beyond.

She tried to swallow, couldn't, her mouth too dry. She started down the steps.


When Longo had all the money laid out on the floor, Taliferro looked at Perry and said, "Go on in. You can pick up your share when you're done."

"Now that's what I call a good deal," Perry said. He went out into the hall. Benny closed his eyes.

Longo was crouched over the money on the floor, counting it again, mouthing silently.

"One million, one hundred and fifty-nine thousand," he said when he was done.

"What's that work out to per man?"

"Straight split?" Longo said.

"Why not?"

"Shouldn't you get more, Danny? I mean, you made this whole thing happen."

"Nah," Taliferro said. "I couldn't have done it without you guys. Five-way split is fair. What's that, about two-forty each?"

"Closer to two-thirty. Nowhere near what we were expecting, though."

"Still," Taliferro said. "Not bad for a few days' work, is it?"

"Not bad at all," Longo said.

She moved down the hall. There were two doors open ahead, light spilling onto the floor. She could hear voices. Two men, maybe three, Taliferro one of them.

Through the second door, she caught a glimpse of tile. A bathroom. At the far end of the corridor, stairs led down. There could be others down there, waiting for her.

At the first door, she heard scuffling inside, a muted groan. She put gloved fingertips against it, eased it open, more of the room coming into view. A mattress on the floor, a scarred spool table, a floor lamp in one corner. On the table was a box of condoms, a leather slapjack, and a chromed automatic.

She opened the door wider. Perry had Marta pinned face-down on the mattress, arms bound behind her, knees on the floor. She was fully clothed, but gagged. She was fighting him, trying to throw him off her, but he was laughing. He pushed her face into the sheet, reached around with his other hand, unsnapped her jeans.

Crissa stepped into the room, tapped the Glock twice against the doorjamb. He froze for a moment, then turned. She aimed the gun at his chest.

"Hoped I'd see you again," he said.

Marta pushed back against him, and he slid into a sitting position on the floor. She twisted away on the mattress, eyes wide with panic. He was still grinning.

"Stand up," Crissa said.

"What if I don't?"

"Then I'll shoot you where you are."

He looked past her, into the hall. "I don't think so."

"You ready to find out?"

He got to his knees, then stood. "Maybe you don't realize the situation here."

"Stay where you are."

Marta rolled off the mattress, scrambled to her feet. Crissa looked at her, then back at Perry. He'd taken a step closer to the table.

"If you're going to reach for that weapon," she said, "go ahead."

"I'm not going to do anything. Except wait. Even if you kill me now, you'll never get out of here alive. You want to shoot me? Go on."

He was right. A shot in here would bring the others, and she had no idea how many there were. Her finger tightened on the trigger.

"Your move," he said.


Longo was dividing up the money. "I may need to break up some of these packs, to make it even."

"Go ahead," Taliferro said.

Longo looked at Benny, winked. "See, if you hadn't been such a greedy prick, you could have had a piece of this."

"That's what I told him," Taliferro said.

When Longo had the money in five piles, he stood, looked down at them. "So, that's what a million dollars looks like."

"That's right," Sal said, raised a revolver from his side, and shot him in the head.

# TWENTY-FIVE

Crissa jumped at the shot. She twisted to look back into the hallway, and then Perry dove for his gun, took the table over with him. She turned back, and he was moving fast, kicking the table away, rolling clear. He came up on one knee, his gun in a two-handed grip, aimed at her chest. She shot him in the throat.

Blood sprayed the mattress. He dropped the gun, went over on his side, hands at his neck. Gasping, he tried to roll away, his face contorted. She kicked his gun into a far corner.

The threat would come from behind her now. To Marta, she said, "Stay here," then went into the hallway, the Glock up. Sal Bruno was coming out of the bathroom, snub-nosed revolver raised. No surprise in his eyes, no expression on his face.

They fired at the same time, the sound of the shots filling the hall. His first bullet splintered the doorjamb by her face. She threw herself back, squeezing the Glock's trigger again and again, casings flying. His left shoulder jerked as if on a wire, and the next two shots hit his chest, pushed him back.

Her feet tangled, and she went down, still firing. Her last two shots went high, one into the wall, the other the ceiling. He took three drunken steps back, face still blank, then fell into the open stairwell.

She rolled onto her knees, then her feet, breathing hard, ears ringing from the shots. How many more of them were up here?

She swung into the bathroom doorway, gun up, took it all in. Benny bound on the black-and-white tile floor. Taliferro standing over him, holding an automatic to his head. Longo slumped facedown near the duffel bag, blood on the wall above him. Money on the floor. Moonlight coming through a window.

Benny met her eyes. She saw the plastic sheeting on the floor, the straight razor and toolbox on the sink, the saw and knives.

Taliferro gripped Benny's collar, twisted the muzzle of the gun into his temple. His knuckle was white on the trigger. She aimed the Glock at his chest, her hands steady.

"I knew you'd come back," Taliferro said. "Knew you wouldn't leave your partner behind."

"That's got nothing to do with it," she said, and fired twice.

The first shot drove him back. The second took him high in the left side of the chest, turned him. He hit the sink, knocked over the toolbox, dropped his gun. He reached out at the last moment, caught the edge of the sink to keep from falling.

He wavered there, looking back at her, and she saw the realization in his eyes. She lowered the Glock. His hand opened slowly, and then there was nothing in his eyes at all. He fell back onto the floor.

She let out her breath.

Benny said, "There's another one downstairs."

She bent, picked up Taliferro's gun, set it on the sink. He lay still, eyes open, unblinking.

She took the razor from the sink, opened it. "Turn around."

Benny rolled to his feet, looked over his shoulder. She sliced through the flex-cuffs.

"Marta," he said.

"In the other room. She's fine. Stay here, until I—," but he was out of the door and down the hall, calling her name.

She went to the stairwell. Bruno lay halfway down the steps, facing the wall. She stepped over him, stooped to get his gun, took the rest of the stairs two at a time. A corridor at the bottom, a doorway on the right that led into the dim bar.

She put the revolver in her pocket, went in with the Glock up, felt the breeze. The front door was open wide. Footsteps outside, slow and clumsy.

She went to the door. A man on crutches was clambering down the sidewalk. She could hear his labored breathing.

He rounded the corner, making for the town car. She followed him. He had his back to her, was fumbling with the crutches, pulling a set of keys from a pants pocket, trying not to fall over.

"Stop," she said, and raised the gun. He froze. A crutch clattered to the street.

Without turning, he said, "Don't shoot me."

"Lose that other crutch. Then come around slowly. Lean back against the car."

He raised his right arm, and the second crutch fell away. He turned and slumped back against the trunk of the Lincoln. He was powerfully built, but his face was pale and wet. She held the front site of the Glock on the V of his open shirt, where a gold cross nestled in chest hair. She could see the butt of a gun in his waistband.

"Not like this," he said. "Please."

She closed the distance, keeping the Glock on him. "Take that out. Slow."

With his weight on the trunk, he pulled the automatic free with two fingers.

"Lose it," she said.

He tossed the gun into the gutter. The chrome finish glinted in the moonlight. She kicked it into a storm drain.

"Any more of you around?" she said.

"What?"

"More of Taliferro's crew. More like you."

His shook his head. He was trying to catch his breath. "Just me."

"Put your hands on the car."

He turned awkwardly, leaned on the trunk. She came up behind, patted him down with her free hand, took the keys from his fingers.

"Danny was going to kill us all," he said. He drew in breath. "Him and Sal. They wanted the money for themselves. No way was he going to split it with us. I knew that."

"You were right." She backed away. "Turn around."

He faced her. "The others?"

She shook her head.

He looked away, weary. Up at the moon, then back at her. "Go ahead."

"Here's the problem," she said. "If I leave you alive, sooner or later, you might decide to come after me, come after that money."

He shook his head. "I won't."

"That's right, you won't. Which leg were you shot in?"

"What?"

"When Roth shot you. Which leg?"

He exhaled, resigned. "Left."

She lowered the Glock, shot him through the right calf. He cried out, went down hard into the gutter. The echo of the shot rolled up the empty street.

She bent, picked up the shell casing. He was moaning, holding on to his leg with both hands.

"Two ways this can go," she said. "I call the paramedics when I'm done here, get you some help. Or I come back and finish it. It's up to you. Understand?"

He squeezed his eyes shut, water leaking out.

"Understand?"

He nodded, face tight with pain. "I understand."

"Then stay where you are. And be quiet."

She looked up and down the street. Dark buildings, shuttered doors, a no-man's-land. No light but the moon high above.

She went back inside.

# TWENTY-SIX

Upstairs, Benny and Marta were in the hallway. He was holding her tight, her head against his shoulder, their faces pale in the over-head light.

"You two all right?" Crissa said.

Benny said, "I think so. Where's Dominic?"

"Outside. He won't bother us. You wait here."

She went past them, into the bedroom. Perry lay where he'd fallen, the floor around him dark with blood. His eyes were open, but there was no movement, no breath.

She knelt, turned her face away, went through his pockets. She found a keychain, drew it out. Ford keys, for the Explorer.

The shell casing from the Glock lay alongside the mattress. She put it in her jacket pocket. Out in the hall, she found six more.

To Benny, she said, "Take a good look around, see if there's anything up here that belongs to either of you. Make sure you get your cell. We don't want to leave anything behind."

She went into the bathroom, stepped over Longo's body, found the last two shell casings. They clinked in her pocket.

The Glock in her belt, she went back downstairs. There were about a dozen liquor bottles on the mirrored rack behind the bar top. A pool table in the middle of the room, cover stretched over it. A dark jukebox in the corner.

She went out, searched both vehicles, looking for anything that would tie them to Benny or her. Dominic had propped himself against the back tire of the Lincoln, was holding his leg, watching her.

In the Explorer, she found two guns in an overnight bag, an envelope full of cash in the glove box. She thumbed through it. Ten grand, maybe. Their traveling money. She left the guns, took the envelope.

No money in the Lincoln. She found another pistol in the trunk wheel well, along with a roadside emergency kit. She opened it. Inside was a can of Fix-A-Flat, two road flares, and a flashlight. She took the flares, shut the trunk.

"What are you going to do?" Dominic said.

She dropped the Lincoln keys into his lap.

"I changed my mind," she said. "You're on your own. Sooner or later, you might be able to get up the strength to get in that car, figure out a way to drive out of here. If not, you can wait for the police. I don't care."

"What do I tell them?"

"That's your business. But if we cross paths again, you'll wish you were back in there with the others. Got that?"

He nodded wearily. "I got it."

She tossed the Explorer keys into the storm drain, left him there, went back inside.

Benny and Marta were down in the bar. He had his arm

around her shoulders. They were huddled together as if for warmth.

"Where's your car?" he said.

"Aren't you forgetting something?"

"I can't go back up there," he said. "She won't go, and I can't leave her alone."

"Are you serious?"

"Please. We're cold."

She told him where the car was. "Stay off the main streets. I'll meet you there, but I need a few minutes."

"Why?"

"Just do it."

When they were gone, she went back upstairs. She pushed Longo's body away, shoveled all the money back into the duffel bag, zipped it shut. She left it near the stairs.

In the bedroom, she pulled the sheet off, used her knife to slice through the mattress. She pulled stuffing out, tried not to look at Perry's body, the pool of blood.

She put the knife away, went back in the hall, took one of the flares from her jacket pocket. She slid off the plastic sheath, reversed the striker cap, got it lit on the second try. It hissed, began to spew sparks and white magnesium smoke. She tossed it onto the mattress. It caught at once, the flames lighting up the room, shadows dancing on the walls.

The hall was filling with smoke. She took a last glance into the bathroom, then picked up the duffel, carried it downstairs, past Bruno's body.

In the bar, she went behind the counter, swept all the bottles onto the floor. They shattered on the wood, contents running together, the smell of it rising up.

She lit the second flare at the door, tossed it over the bar top into the pool of alcohol. It blazed up blue and yellow, flames tracing the path along the floor where the liquor had flowed. The bar mirror reflected their light. Smoke began to gather beneath the pressed tin ceiling.

She slung the bag over her shoulder, went out, left the door open to feed the flames.

A block away, she felt the first tremor. It started in her right hand, spread up her arm. She opened and closed her hand, felt the muscles spasm and flutter. She was shaking. She squeezed her fist tight until it stopped, turned to look back.

The first-floor windows of the Victory were illuminated from within, a leaping red glow like a thing alive. Upstairs, smoke was seeping from the boarded-up windows, flames creeping along the edges of the plywood.

One of the first-floor windows popped and collapsed, flames licking out. The torn awning caught, began to smoke. Flames sprang up, the faded lettering turning black, then disappearing. The entire awning went up almost all at once, the glow of it lighting storefronts along the street.

When she reached the car, they were waiting there together. She dropped the duffel at their feet. "This belongs to you," she said. "It's what it was all about, remember?"

Benny looked down at it. Neither of them moved.

"Take it," Crissa said. "It's yours. You earned it. No one's going to come looking for it anymore. If you don't take it, I will."

Smoke was drifting up over the buildings, past the moon, high into the sky. She heard the first sirens, coming from somewhere deeper in Brooklyn.

"Make up your mind," she said. "We're running out of time."

"She's right," Marta said.

Benny looked at her. "What?"

"Take it."

"Smart girl," Crissa said. "Let's go."

Their first stop was Bay Ridge, to get the Honda. It was a block away from what would be a homicide scene. If anyone ran the plates, it would be a link back to her.

When Benny and Marta got out, Crissa said, "Meet me down at the house. I have to make a stop first. If you get there before me, just wait."

Benny looked dazed, tired.

"You okay to drive?" she said.

"I don't know."

Marta said, "I'll drive."

"Good," Crissa said. Then to Benny, "You want to take that duffel with you?"

He looked at the trunk, then back at her, shook his head. "No. I trust you. And after all this, I don't want to get stopped in Brooklyn, have some nosy cop find it."

"Smart."

"Getting there," he said.

Halfway across the upper level of the Verrazano, she pulled over, put her hazards on. It was 3:00 A.M., the traffic sparse.

She left the engine running, got out. Cold up here, wind whining around the suspension cables. She could feel the road-way sway beneath her. In the distance, back the way she'd come, a pulsing light, thin smoke drifting past the moon.

A car flew by in the opposite lane, a blur of metal and light. She stepped over the guardrail to the outer railing. Now she could see the water some five hundred feet below, the blue light of the bridge reflected on its surface.

There would be surveillance cameras up here, maybe someone watching her even now. She would have to be quick.

She held the Glock below her waist, ejected the magazine, and dropped it into darkness. Then she disassembled the gun by feel, tossed the pieces out into the void. The shell casings were next, the wind catching them almost as soon as they left her hand. They clinked against the metal supports, disappeared.

A car blew past her, horn blaring. She tossed Benny's phone, then her own. Their last links to what had happened at the Victory.

Another car sped by, narrowly missing the Taurus. Enough risk for tonight, she thought. Time to go home.

She got back in the car, killed the hazards, put her signal on. She waited for a car to pass, then pulled out after it. The darkness of Staten Island ahead, then Jersey. Brooklyn behind her, a red glow in the night.

# TWENTY-SEVEN

She woke just after dawn, aching all over, and with a deep soreness in her hips. But the pain in her stomach was gone.

She made coffee, drank it in the kitchen, giving them time to sleep. When she was done, it was after eight. She knocked lightly on the bedroom door.

After a moment, Benny opened it. He looked ten years older, his eyes red beneath the glasses. Behind him, Marta lay asleep on the still-made bed, fully dressed, her back to them. The duffel bag was on the floor.

She motioned for him to come out. He closed the door gently behind him.

"Time to be on the road," she said. "The sooner the better. I'll drive you. Where were you headed?"

"New Haven. To catch a train."

"I'll take you. But that duffel's no good for traveling. It'll attract too much attention. Use these." She nodded at the two new suitcases on the floor. She'd emptied them out, put all her money back in the other duffel.

"Put some clothes on top in each, enough to pass a casual inspection," she said. "When you get where you're going, do what I said—salt some away in safe deposit boxes. That way you know you've got a stake somewhere if things go sour. What you do with the rest is up to you."

"Thanks. What about the car?"

"I'll take care of that." She looked at her watch. "I want to be out of here in an hour."

"All right." He looked back at the bedroom door.

"She can sleep on the train," Crissa said. "Better for both of you to be on the move."

"It was a rough night for her."

"For all of us," she said.

At noon, they were in New Haven. The sky was gray, rain spotting the windshield. Crissa steered the Honda to the curb outside Union Station. There were cars ahead of her, a taxi queue to the left. Benny and Marta were in the backseat, their suitcases in the trunk. Her own duffel was back there, too. It felt safer to have it with her.

"Let me go inside and see what the schedules are," he said. "I'll leave our bags here, be right back."

"All right," Crissa said.

He opened the door, touched Marta on the shoulder. "Wait here, baby. I'll be back in a sec."

Crissa watched him go inside, people streaming around him. She looked at Marta in the rearview. "You have family?"

"Parents. In Indiana."

"You going back to see them?"

"Someday. Benny says we need to get settled somewhere else first. Then we'll find a way."

Crissa watched the front entrance. They'd passed the New Haven police station less than a block away. She had a sudden image of cops coming out the doors of the terminal, surrounding the Honda, guns out.

"Is that right?" Marta said. "What you said last night? About nobody looking for us anymore?"

"Probably."

"That's not very reassuring."

"Maybe not. But it'll have to do."

Benny came back out, a ticket envelope in his hand. Crissa powered down the passenger window. He leaned in, said, "We're in luck. There's an Amtrak leaving in twenty-five minutes for—"

"I don't want to know," she said.

He looked at her for a moment, then smiled. "All right, then."

She popped the trunk, got out. Benny set the first suitcase on the curb. He looked around. "Where are all the redcaps?"

"Wrong decade," she said. She pulled the second one out. When all four bags were lined up at the curb, she said, "Wait a minute."

Her back to them, she leaned into the trunk, unzipped her duffel, took out the black velvet bag with the red drawstring, the diamond necklace and bracelet inside.

She lobbed it at him. He caught it in front of his chest.

"What's this?" he said.

"Wedding present. Keep them, sell them, whatever. They're yours."

He weighed the bag in his hand, looked at Marta, then back at Crissa. "Thanks."

"You're going to miss your train. And you'll want to keep an eye on those suitcases. Be a shame to lose them at this point."

"You're right," he said.

Marta looked at her. "Thank you."

"Go somewhere far away," Crissa said. "Keep your head down. Stay safe."

He bounced the bag in his hand. "Then I guess this is it. Again."

"It is." She shut the trunk lid.

"Like I said, I wish I'd known you back in—"

"Your train."

"Right." He put the bag in a coat pocket, picked up two of the suitcases. "I guess we'll be seeing you."

"No," Crissa said. "You won't."

She watched them go into the station together, carrying their bags, but staying close, shoulder to shoulder. She stood there for a while. Then she got back behind the wheel.


She returned the Honda at an agency near Newark Airport, got them to call a limo to take her back to Avon.

She waited on a plastic chair in the office, watching rivulets of rain on the plate glass, the duffel at her feet. When the limo drew up, she hoisted the bag, went out.

The driver got out, opened the trunk, reached for the bag.

"No," she said. "I've got it."

"Okay, ma'am," he said. He was dark-skinned, had a lilting African accent. "It's up to you."

He shut the trunk again, opened the rear door. She put the duffel on the seat, got in after it.

Heading south on the Turnpike, she saw he was watching her

in the rearview. She knew how she must look. She was exhausted, sore. She'd sleep for a few hours, then bring Jimmy his money, and call Rathka. See about a plane ticket to Texas.

"Excuse me, ma'am," he said. "But that's most unusual."

"What?"

"That bag you are carrying. It's not a ladies' bag at all. No good for clothes, I would not think. I have never seen a woman like you carrying one."

"Is that right?"

"Yes. It's something a man would carry. A sailor maybe, or soldier. But I don't think you're either of those, are you?"

"No, I'm not."

"You are a serious person, though. I can tell."

She didn't respond, looked out the window at the traffic passing by, the sound of the wipers lulling her. She felt herself drifting.

"So," he said.

She opened her eyes. He was watching her again. "What?"

"Forgive me for asking, I know it is none of my business, but you have made me curious."

"About what?"

"The bag. What is in it?"

She met his eyes in the rearview. "A million dollars."

He laughed, nodded. "A million dollars. How is it they say? Oh, yes. 'Good one.'" He laughed again. "A million dollars. Very good, indeed."

# TWENTY-EIGHT

Back home, she dropped the duffel on the floor, broke out a new cell from its plastic packaging. She activated it, punched in Rathka's number.

Monique answered. "Miss Hendryx, I think Mister Rathka's been trying to reach you. Please hold."

Crissa carried the phone to the sliding glass door, opened the blinds. Rain pocked the surface of the inlet, the water gray and churning, the same color as the sky. In her mind, she saw blackened, twisted embers smoking in the rain, grinning skulls buried in ash.

When Rathka came on the line, he said, "I've tried calling you. There was no answer."

"I switched phones. What's wrong?"

A pause on the other end of the line. Silence. She felt her stomach tighten. "Tell me."

"It's our friend in Texas. Something happened."

"What?"

"That situation I told you about, with another inmate. It came to a head. In a bad way."

She closed her eyes, drew in breath. "Is he dead?"

"No. He's a little beat up, but he'll be okay, as far as that goes. What I know, I got from our guard. Apparently, there were some threats made yesterday afternoon by that other inmate. Made where others could hear them. Our friend didn't respond, just went back to his cell. Then last night, right before lockdown, he went down to where this other inmate was playing cards, in the common room. He had a knife made from a bed spring. At least, that's what they're saying."

She breathed in, out. "What happened?"

"They got into it right there. In front of witnesses, a pair of guards, security cameras, the whole thing."

"Did Wayne kill him?" Conscious she had used his name for the first time, not caring.

"No, but close. They medevaced the inmate out to a hospital not far from the facility. I checked earlier today. He's still in intensive care."

"Will he live?"

"No one knows right now."

"What about the hearing?"

Rathka didn't answer. There was no need to.

She felt light-headed, moved to the couch, sat. She had a vision of Wayne walking down the tier, moving toward his fate, taking control of it, not letting his future be decided by someone else.

We were so close, baby, she thought. So close.

She opened her eyes, felt the water there, blinked it away.

"I'm sorry," Rathka said.

"He did it for me."

"What?"

"He told me I should move on. That I should forget him. That it was better that way."

She looked at the tattoo on the inside of her wrist. You were wrong, baby, she thought. You were wrong, wrong, wrong.

"Are you still there?" Rathka said.

"Yeah." She looked out at the rain.

"I'm expecting some more news from our guard soon. Maybe something about the other inmate's condition. I'll let you know as soon as I do."

"It doesn't matter anyway. Not anymore."

"What's that?"

"Never mind. Let me know what you find out. I'll have this number for a few days."

"I will. And again, I'm sorry."

"I am, too," she said, and ended the call.

She sat on the couch, watched rain sluice down the sliding glass door, listened to it drum on the roof. The duffel full of money was at her feet, the bag with Jimmy's cut beside it. She would take it to him tomorrow maybe, tell him everything that had happened. Tell him about Wayne.

For months, she'd lived with the hope that with enough money, enough luck, he would be out of there, back with her. Then, one day, Maddie, too. The three of them together at last, a family. All of that gone now.

Wind rattled the glass. A low howl filled the room.

But she was through running. Through waiting for something that was never going to come, that she couldn't have. This was her life now. Not something in the future she could put together, piece by piece, like a puzzle, trying to make everything fit.

This was it. There was nothing else. And no more running. If anyone came looking for her, they could find her here.

She took out the Tomcat, eased back the slide to check the chambered shell. It was a good weapon after all, solid, dependable. She set it on the arm of the couch.

Rain blew against the glass. She put a hand over the cold gun. Tomorrow she'd call Rathka back, set up that new account for Maddie, start moving money around. She had enough of it now, all she needed for the moment. Enough to buy a new name, a new set of papers, a start on a new life.

But that was tomorrow. Right now there was just the gray sky, the wind, the darkening room, the bag of cash at her feet, the gun under her hand. All she had in the world. All she might ever have. And not enough.